She watched detail of the room—*especially her.*

She shivered and recalled her explosive reaction to the innocent touch of her fingers against Tanner's skin. Not a problem. She'd keep her hands away from him and on her work, and keep her mind on her promise to Mr. Frank.

A detail in the investigator's report popped into her head: While Tanner had no shortage of women in his life, he either couldn't keep them, or didn't want to, since no relationship ever lasted more than a couple of months.

Why had that little morsel surfaced? He wasn't even her type.

She could so easily picture Tanner at home in Fairfax House. New Haven would embrace him, give him the sense of belonging and roots he had lost since his parents died. The fact that she could see it wasn't enough, though—*he* had to, also....

Dear Reader,

Brr... February's below-freezing temperatures call for a mug of hot chocolate, a fuzzy afghan and a heartwarming book from Silhouette Romance. Our books will heat you to the tips of your toes with the sizzling sexual tension that courses between our stubborn heroes and the determined heroines who ultimately melt their hardened hearts.

In Judy Christenberry's *Least Likely To Wed*, her sinfully sexy cowboy hero has his plans for lifelong bachelorhood foiled by the searing kisses of a spirited single mom. While in Sue Swift's *The Ranger & the Rescue*, an amnesiac cowboy stakes a claim on the heart of a flame-haired heroine—but will the fires of passion still burn when he regains his memory?

Tensions reach the boiling point in Raye Morgan's *She's Having My Baby!*—the final installment of the miniseries HAVING THE BOSS'S BABY—when our heroine discovers just who fathered her baby-to-be.... And tempers flare in Rebecca Russell's *Right Where He Belongs*, in which our handsome hero must choose between his cold plan for revenge and a woman's warm and tender love.

Then simmer down with the incredibly romantic heroes in Teresa Southwick's *What If We Fall In Love?* and Colleen Faulkner's *A Shocking Request*. You'll laugh, you'll cry, you'll fall in love all over again with these deeply touching stories about widowers who get a second chance at love.

So this February, come in from the cold and warm your heart and spirit with one of these temperature-raising books from Silhouette Romance. Don't forget the marshmallows!

Happy reading!

Mary-Theresa Hussey

Mary-Theresa Hussey
Senior Editor

Please address questions and book requests to:
Silhouette Reader Service
U.S.: 3010 Walden Ave., P.O. Box 1325, Buffalo, NY 14269
Canadian: P.O. Box 609, Fort Erie, Ont. L2A 5X3

Right Where He Belongs

REBECCA RUSSELL

SILHOUETTE *Romance*®

Published by Silhouette Books

America's Publisher of Contemporary Romance

To my parents, who have always believed in me.
To my husband, son and daughter, for sacrificing along with me in order to make my dream come true. To my friends, especially Vicki, who never wavered in support and faith in me. And to my great-aunt Ruthie, who inspired this book with her wonderful stories about the past.

 SILHOUETTE BOOKS

ISBN 0-373-19575-3

RIGHT WHERE HE BELONGS

Copyright © 2002 by Rebecca Russell

Visit Silhouette at www.eHarlequin.com

Printed in U.S.A.

REBECCA RUSSELL

Between racquetball, hockey, volunteering, writing and family, Rebecca Russell is an "at home" mom who is rarely home! She lives with her husband of nineteen years and a teenage son and daughter in Plano, Texas. Although grounded in her suburban life and small-town Ohio roots, Rebecca loves to spend time with flawed but heroic characters who find love and a happy ending.

Rebecca loves to hear from readers. You can write to her at P.O. Box 852125, Richardson, TX 75085-2125, or e-mail her at rebecca_russell_22@yahoo.com.

Dear Reader,

For most of my life, I was content to devour books the way some people binge on chocolate. Writing proved as natural as breathing, but remained personal and private.

I had no idea that fateful night when I walked into a creative writing class at a local community college that my life would never be the same. After all, I was only looking for something fun to do. The class was actually "How To Write a Novel," and the instructor, a romance author. She saw something in my writing and insisted I attend a local writer's conference. Once there, she took me under her wing and within hours I was hooked.

Years later, I told that same instructor/author that I didn't know if I wanted to thank her or curse her. I was thrilled to have a dream, but frustrated by how long it was taking to make that dream come true. And just like the single woman who swears off men soon meets the love of her life, when I had decided to worry less about getting published and write because I love to write, I sold! Getting the call from Silhouette Romance was one of the most exciting moments of my life and proof that dreams shouldn't come with expiration dates.

I can't imagine anything more rewarding than writing about the power of love. My hope is that as you read *Right Where He Belongs*, you'll become so involved in Cassie and Tanner's struggle to find true happiness and love, that hours will go by and seem like minutes; when you return to your life with all its challenges and joys, you'll be ready to do some dreaming of your own.

Rebecca Russell

Chapter One

"It's payback time," Tanner Fairfax said softly, hoping somehow his deceased grandfather could hear him and know the intentions of his only grandchild.

At the soonest possible moment, Tanner planned to sign over the deed to Fairfax House to the highest bidder, the exact thing his grandfather would have hated. Sweet, poetic justice for himself, and his parents, the people his grandfather had hurt the most.

The family estate claimed the corner lot of prime property in the sleepy farm town of New Haven, Ohio. The old but elegant two-story mansion reminded him of an aging queen who refused to budge from her throne of power. A well-maintained barn stood like a sentry next to the house.

The hot July sun bounced off a massive bay window. He shielded his eyes with one hand to get a better look. Someone had obviously been busy. A pristine white exterior explained the odor of fresh paint that coated the humid air. The excellent condition of the wraparound porch suggested recent repairs.

He hesitated at the bottom of the steps leading to his family's estate, overcome by a sudden wariness. Painful memories of his one and only visit as a naive, excited five-year-old boy threatened to surface, but he pushed them away. He was a grown man now, in control of his own destiny.

No tears today.

Tanner took the porch steps two at a time. He grabbed the key from the back pocket of his worn jeans, opened the heavy front door and stepped inside.

Cool darkness greeted him, a startling contrast to the midday sunshine he'd left outside. He found a switch, and with a flick, light sprinkled downward from an ornate chandelier. A thick Oriental rug covered the hardwood floor. Impressive, but not important.

From the back of the house, a clattering erupted and he froze. "Who's there?" he called out.

He made his way toward the sound, cautious, but not frightened. He knew little about small towns, but doubted he'd find much to fear. Anyone who owned and managed a construction company could certainly handle getting rid of an uninvited guest.

"I'm in the kitchen, Mr. Fairfax," a feminine voice answered. "Just walk straight ahead."

So, the stranger was a woman. Another surprise. He passed by a blur of rooms on either side as he followed the clamor to the sliver of light that escaped beneath a door at the end of the hall. He opened the door and detected an almost sweet, oddly familiar odor. An herb? A spice?

No matter. He stepped inside. The intended curt "hello" died on his lips. In the midst of the spacious kitchen stood a tall, slender woman dressed in white, paint-splattered bib overalls. Wisps of mahogany-brown hair escaped from a painter's cap. Dark-green eyes sparkled and her hundred-watt smile knocked the breath out of him.

With an intensity he couldn't help but admire, she vigorously wiped down scratched cupboards painted a murky brown. The same dreary color had been forced onto the paneling that covered the bottom half of the walls. Faded, water-stained wallpaper drooped in one corner. Tools littered the countertops. A large bucket and mop hugged a corner; several folded tarps dotted the floor.

"Who are you and how did you get in?" he finally managed to ask.

"I can explain, Mr. Fairfax."

The warm friendliness in her voice erased all other questions from his mind, beckoned him to move closer to her, but he stood his ground as she side-stepped the bucket, mop and tarps.

"I'm Cassie Leighton, owner of Leighton's Custom Remodeling. Your grandfather hired me to do repairs before he died."

She held out her hand, then pulled it back, an apologetic grin on her face. No wedding ring, he noted, for no other reason than habit. "Sorry," she said, then grabbed a rag out of a back pocket and wiped her hands. "I didn't know I was such a mess."

Surprise hit Tanner hard. He had actually been eager to discover if the touch of her hand packed the same wallop as her smile. Maybe he was coming down with the flu or something.

''Mr. Fairfax?''

He took a much needed deep breath, confused by the fact that his earlier annoyance over an intruder had vanished. ''How did you know it was me out front and not some burglar?'' he asked, more comfortable with suspicion than his strange reaction to a woman he'd just met.

''Not much crime in New Haven. And the minute you arrived at Mr. Samuels's office, his secretary beeped me and I rushed over.'' She openly studied him from the top of his head, to his T-shirt, faded jeans and scuffed boots. ''She warned me that you looked just like your dad.''

Her intensity reminded him of his own when he examined a piece of wood for knots or uneven grain. He wondered if he measured up, then just as quickly dismissed the notion. He'd always taken the comparison as a compliment, so why doubt it now? Besides, it wasn't as if he had trouble getting a date when he wanted one.

He was just unnerved from hearing a complete stranger talk about his father as if she'd known him, Tanner reasoned, which was impossible. Both of his parents had been dead for so long now that he could hardly remember the sound of their voices and other details he thought he'd never forget.

''Yep, you definitely have the Fairfax hair and eyes,'' Cassie said, still smiling.

A sign he had passed inspection and wouldn't be tossed into the scrap pile? ''Why wasn't I warned someone would be here?'' he asked, annoyed he cared at all about what a stranger thought of him, even if the stranger happened to have a natural beauty that made him think of hayrides and campfires.

Wait a minute. He'd never gone on a hayride, let alone shared a campfire with a woman.

Crazy thoughts. Not like him at all. Lack of sleep, he reasoned. The long drive from Texas had left him punchy.

"Mr. Samuels might not have realized his secretary beeped me. She knows how I feel about this house. We thought you were arriving tomorrow, so I had planned on cleaning up tonight."

Tanner shrugged. "I ended up leaving Tyler early and drove straight through."

"You don't have much of an accent for someone from Texas."

"I guess it's because neither of my parents had one. Is it a problem that I arrived early?"

"No problem at all. It's just that I—" A muted ringing interrupted Cassie. She reached deep into a bib pocket, pulled out a cellular phone and checked the I.D. of the caller. "Excuse me, but I've been trying to reach this guy all morning," she explained. Her long, slender fingers gripped the small phone next to her ear. He wasn't surprised to see short, unpolished nails that were as practical as her overalls.

Most women he came across would just as soon run or hide from the prospect of getting dirty, but Cassie had chosen a profession that almost demanded it. He imagined such a woman could get ready for a date in no time; wouldn't think twice about ruining her makeup and hair for the chance to walk in the rain.

Damn. What was it about Cassie that made him think such foreign, mushy thoughts? As for how she might behave on a date, he'd never know and didn't care. He had a game plan: get in, settle a score, get out. No complications.

In need of a distraction, he focused on Cassie's phone conversation. Impolite, sure, but his peace of mind mattered more at the moment.

"No, Mike, that won't do," Cassie insisted. "We promised to have all the fixtures in by tomorrow, even if it is Saturday. Call Danny in. He could use the extra money, but don't bother asking Georgie. I told her she could leave early for her daughter's soccer game. I'll stop by the site later."

Tanner appreciated the firm way she dealt with her employee, although he was surprised she knew so much personal detail about her workers. Turnover was high in construction; remembering just the last names of his transient employees proved a challenge.

She punched a button and slid the phone back into its hiding place. "Sorry for the interruption, Mr. Fairfax. Anyway, it's wonderful that you're here. And don't worry about the mess," she added, as if she could read the doubt in his mind. "I'll be done cleaning up in no time. This really is a beautiful house."

Cassie's gaze turned somber and she put her hand on his arm. "I'm sorry about your grandfather."

Her cool fingers created a heat in his body to rival the scorching sun of a Texas summer. He stiffened, too surprised by the incredible chemistry to move. How could a gesture, obviously meant to comfort, set him on fire?

No. He didn't want her unexpected touch and kind words, and he definitely didn't want anything or anyone to complicate his stay in New Haven.

"Mr. Frank liked to huff and puff a lot, but he was

a pussycat inside." Her eyes glistened with unshed tears.

"Or a lion." Time had failed to soften Tanner's memory of the old man with the fierce eyes and bellowing voice. His grandfather had acted as if he were king of the jungle; he demanded compliance and punished those who dared to defy him.

Cassie quickly pulled her hand away from Tanner's arm, stunned to discover that touching him had the effect of tossing a match on turpentine. She shouldn't have been surprised, though. His dark good looks had already thrown her off balance. He had hair the color of wrought iron and his eyes were Gondola Blue. The deep, rich color, her favorite, made her long for a romantic getaway to Venice where she'd ride a gondola with her lover....

"Anyway," she continued, desperate to organize her thoughts. "Your grandfather arranged to have the exterior painted, the porch and roof repaired and the new kitchen floor installed." She nervously gestured toward the sink. "He insisted that this room be functional before you arrived, knew he didn't—didn't have much time left," she said, her voice faltering.

Darn it. She swore she wouldn't get all weepy. But she missed the old coot who'd been her mentor as well as her friend.

She took a deep breath and stacked the tarps near the door, then slid tools into the numerous pockets of her overalls. "Would you like me to clear this all out each day, or leave it?"

"Leave it. The job will go quicker."

"Okay. If you don't mind a little clutter and dust, this room is useable. Or you can use the dining room as a makeshift kitchen until I'm done."

"How long?" He gestured around the room. "I don't want anything to interfere with my plans for a quick sell."

Cassie flinched. "It sounds like you made up your mind before you even saw the house."

"You've got that right."

Tanner was obviously going to make her other job difficult. Just before he had died, Mr. Frank had confided in her the details of his regretful past. He had made it very clear that he alone had ruined Tanner's chance to know and feel a part of his family's history. Cassie had a hard time believing Mr. Frank could've ever acted so vengefully, but the pain in his eyes told the truth. "Sounds pretty ungrateful to me," she challenged. "Your grandfather didn't have to leave you the house and—"

"I'm sure there was the usual selfish reason behind it."

Tanner couldn't be more wrong. Until his final breath, Mr. Frank had hoped that his pleading letters to his grandson would bring forgiveness and a chance to meet. But time had run out.

Mr. Frank had asked her to spend the thirty days trying to convince Tanner to forgive his grandfather, in order to accept his birthright. This was one promise she intended to keep.

"If you think you can't make the deadline, Ms. Leighton, I'll get someone else on the job."

She would *not* let him rattle her. "Call me Cassie, and don't worry. I'll be done in plenty of time. Ten to fourteen days, depending on what you want done. I'm sure you have other business to take care of first, so if it's okay with you, I'll come by tomorrow and strip the wallpaper."

"On Saturday?"

She shrugged. "It's one of my busiest days. Just keep in mind, if you want any painting done in here, that's done first. Then the walls will have to be prepped, so it could be a couple of days to a week before we put up the new wallpaper. During that time you can go over paint and paper samples. We can meet at my office downtown or I can bring them here."

He stared at her in confusion. "Me? What do I have to do with it?"

"You can make any changes to the house you want to. Your grandfather gave you authorization so you wouldn't have to wait the thirty days."

"It's bad enough I have to live in this house for a month before I can unload it. I don't care what you do about any wallpaper or paint."

She produced a broom from a closet, a task she'd performed many times before. Grateful to have something in her hands, she restored order to the room. While she worked, she stole glances at the tall, handsome man with the lean, yet muscular build.

Mr. Frank had shown her several grainy photos of his grandson along with a written report provided by the private investigator hired to keep tabs on Tanner over the years. But a picture didn't reveal intensity or Tanner's true essence.

"Hold on. How did you know about the live-in clause?"

Cassie heard the cold, quiet strength behind his casual question. She shivered. He might look like his father, but he had his grandfather's suspicious nature.

"Your grandfather told me. But even if he hadn't, New Haven has an incredible grapevine. Rule number one in a small town—no secrets allowed. You'll get used to it after a while, Mr. Fairfax.''

"Call me Tanner. Mr. Fairfax was my dad. And I won't be here long enough to get used to anything."

We'll see about that. Tanner might have *outsider* written all over him—the way he carried himself, the way he had flinched when she'd touched his arm, the guarded look in his eyes—but he belonged in New Haven; he belonged at Fairfax House. He just didn't know it yet.

Cassie knew firsthand how a sense of roots provided emotional comfort, because she'd been given such a gift. The town, its people, were home. If Mr. Frank hadn't disowned his son, Tanner would have been born and raised in New Haven and received the blessing of roots as well.

Mr. Frank had insisted that Cassie was the only person who could help him right such a wrong, since she couldn't imagine being happy anywhere else.

A person made of stone might have refused to help. She, on the other hand, was made up entirely of mush. Mush, with a grain of selfishness. Deep down, she knew that she had agreed to help for another reason. Years ago, she had failed to keep a promise she'd made to her father just before he died. Finally, she had a chance to prove her word meant something.

She watched Tanner as he noted every detail of the room, including her. Especially her. She shivered again and recalled her explosive reaction earlier to the innocent touch of her fingers against Tanner's skin. Not a problem. She'd keep her hands away from him and on her work, and keep her mind on her promise to Mr. Frank.

A detail in the investigator's report popped into her head: while Tanner had no shortage of women in his life, he either couldn't keep them, or didn't want to, since no relationship ever lasted more than a couple of months.

Why had that little morsel surfaced? He wasn't even her type. She preferred easygoing and quick to smile.

"This place will need updating in order to sell," Tanner said, a welcome interruption to her disturbing train of thought. "I want to get moving on this. Since you're coming tomorrow anyway, go ahead and bring samples of what's hot right now."

She frowned as she brushed her fingertips over the faded, water-stained wallpaper. Such a grand house deserved more than the latest color or decorating fad. But the new owner's determination to take the money and run concerned her more.

She could easily picture Tanner at home in Fairfax House. New Haven would embrace him, give him the sense of belonging and roots he had lost since his parents died. The fact she could see it wasn't enough, though—*he* had to, also.

"Unless you have more important jobs," Tanner added dryly.

She knew what she'd like to do with the sample books. Maybe a bonk on the head would make him realize what a gift he'd been given. Too bad she couldn't afford to alienate him. "Of course not. I'll see if I can get the books back from a customer. And for your information, Mr. Samuels asked me to make this house a priority, but I would've made it one anyway. This house is special to me. I practically grew up here."

Tanner's dark eyes narrowed. "Are you a relative?"

"Heavens, no. Just a pesky kid who hung around." She sighed and inhaled the familiar, heartwarming scent she would forever associate with Fairfax House.

Tears threatened to form once again but she refused to cry. She had to remain strong in order to gain the new owner's confidence. "I love that smell, don't you?"

Tanner sniffed the air. "I can't place it. What is it?"

"Vanilla. Your grandfather simmered some on the stove every day, and whenever I'm here I do the same thing. He said it reminded him of your grandmother. Did you know she was only sixty when she died? Cancer. But she didn't suffer long." Mr. Frank, though, had never recovered from his loss.

Love certainly didn't come with any guarantees. Cassie's father had died of a heart attack at thirty-four, leaving her mother without the love of her life way too soon. Cassie had no intention of wasting time when she found The One. They would live, play and work together, a concept a man like Tanner would never understand. He obviously preferred to love 'em and leave 'em, if one could believe the reports from the investigator. "I teased Mr. Frank that they made vanilla candles and air fresheners, but he said they weren't the same. I sure miss him."

Cassie blinked back the tears, reminded afresh of the pain of losing her dear friend. A friend she refused to let down. "I'll see you in the morning, Tanner, around nine," she said, and left through the back door of the kitchen.

Tanner watched Cassie disappear, her eyes shimmering with unshed tears. He'd never met a woman who wore her emotions so close to the surface. No doubt about it, she'd taken the old man's death hard.

Tanner couldn't imagine his rigid grandfather simmering vanilla for a wife long gone. The ice water in his veins wouldn't allow such a sentimental ritual.

What had Cassie seen in such an old, manipulative person? Tanner could only think of two explanations: she was just another one of his victims, or a schemer who had gained more than a repair job from the old man.

Tanner made a mental note to check the details of his grandfather's will. He had no living relatives. Although he wasn't the sole beneficiary, he couldn't remember Cassie's name on the list.

He'd been warned that small towns had no secrets, so he shouldn't have much trouble finding out more about Cassie. Suspicion was good. Anything was better than dwelling on why he'd felt such relief at discovering she wasn't a relative.

He didn't want any complications. For the next thirty days he intended to relax. A former boss, retired and bored, had jumped at the chance to fill in as manager, so for once, the lengthy time away from his company didn't present a problem.

He'd spend his time getting a feel for what his truck-driver dad's life must have been like growing up in New Haven, Ohio. From what little he knew, things hadn't soured for his dad until he defied his father and left town after high school graduation.

Tanner's mind wondered back to how familiar Cassie seemed with the house. She'd fetched a broom as if she'd done so many times before, had known of his grandfather's habits and the conditions of the will.

For some reason the familiarity, imagined or not, bothered him. His reaction made no sense whatsoever. *He* was the one who had ignored every bribe and turned down all invitations to come live in Fairfax House.

Tanner refused to waste another minute on the confusion he felt over being in the huge, dark house again.

"Yoo-hoo," yelled a high-pitched voice from the front of the house. Rapid pounding followed.

"Now what?" Tanner muttered, and left to answer the front door. He gave the rooms he passed along the way a cursory glance. Elegantly curved furniture filled the formal living room and dining room. Pictures in old-looking frames covered the top of a buffet. To his left, he noted a den that had obviously been turned into a bedroom. He'd stash his gear there, later.

He opened the door and discovered a woman with orange hair piled on top of her head, wearing enough makeup to start her own cosmetics business. Oven mitts covered her hands. Steam escaped from a glass dish of green beans. He took a whiff of the unmistakable aroma of cream of mushroom soup and dried onions and his mouth watered.

"I want to be the first to officially welcome you." The woman smiled, ducked under his arm that held open the door and zeroed in on the kitchen.

He blinked, floored by the idea that a stranger had just bulldozed her way inside, then quickly followed.

"We're so sorry about your grandfather," the stranger said. She placed the dish on one of the burners on the stove and shoved the mitts into apron pockets. "But we're just tickled to have another Fairfax in this house. It's Tanner, isn't it?"

"Yes, but—"

"I'm Mrs. Boone, from across the street." He shook her offered hand. "Mr. Boone would've come, too, but he's recovering from surgery and can't get around just yet. Your grandfather loved my green bean casserole, so I just know you'll love it, too. And if you have any questions about New Haven, I'm the town historian. I've lived here all my life, so I've seen it all."

"Thanks, but I won't be here—"

"Why, you're the spitting image of your daddy. Frankie was quite the charmer." She leaned toward Tanner. "Not at all like your grandfather. That Frank, Sr. was short on charm, but he was fair and a man of his word."

Tanner was already weary of the praise for a man who must have hidden his shortcomings from the town. "I see. Well, thanks again, Mrs. Boone."

"You're more than welcome. Tell me, are you as full of pluck as your daddy was? 'Cause this town could use shaking up."

"Frankie, you're finally home," a feeble voice called out from behind the screen of the kitchen door. A stooped, white-haired woman shuffled inside.

Mrs. Boone placed her hand on the old woman's elbow. "Oh, no, Mrs. Johnson. Frankie and Susan passed away years ago in that horrible car accident, remember?"

"Nonsense, child. I'd know that hair and those eyes anywhere. Why did you stay away so long, Frankie?"

A mixture of emotions jackhammered Tanner. The warmth and joy in the stranger's voice, the lines of concern and compassion on her face, and the fact that she'd obviously known and liked his father caused Tanner's throat to grow tight. He swallowed hard. Until that moment, he hadn't realized how much he craved to know the details of his parents' childhoods.

"The town hasn't been the same since you left, dear boy."

Tanner had no idea how to respond to the woman without confusing her more, so he played along. He smiled. "How have you been, Mrs. Johnson?"

She sighed. "Teaching isn't what it used to be. No respect, no joy of learning. Your daddy thought you could scare kids into doing the right thing, or at the very least bribe them. But I daresay I disagree. Where is the rascal, anyway?"

A sad smile crossed Mrs. Boone's face. "Mrs. Johnson was the best math teacher New Haven High ever had. She lives just across the alley. On her good days she liked to come over to spar with your grandfather. You could hear those two all the way downtown. Obviously, today isn't a good day. Come on, Mrs. Johnson, I'll walk you home."

Tanner looked forward to a good day when they could go back in time together. "I'll drop by for a visit sometime, if that's okay with you, Mrs. Johnson."

"Any time, dear boy. It's time I have plenty of."

Mrs. Boone led the stooped woman toward the door. "Oh, look, Tanner!" Mrs. Boone said over her shoulder. "You've got more company. And you're in luck. Looks like Miss Eva brought cinnamon rolls. One whiff, and you'll agree they're to die for."

His warm, nostalgic mood evaporated at the sight of several strangers approaching the house. He worried he was caught in the *Father Knows Best* version of *The Twilight Zone*. What else explained why strangers felt free to wander into his house, or why people admired a jerk like his grandfather?

No matter. *He* knew the man for what he really was—a scheming, coldhearted tyrant.

Every citizen in New Haven could line up at his door with gifts and kind words about his grandfather. Tanner didn't care; he'd ignore them all.

And he for damn sure wouldn't give in to any interest or attraction he might feel toward Cassie Leighton.

Chapter Two

Cassie cradled the grocery sacks against her chest and hurried across the street. A quick glance at Tanner's truck revealed it hadn't budged since she'd left Fairfax House earlier that afternoon. A single light in the old house led her to believe he was home. Good. She hated to think she'd wasted time deciding what to wear for nothing. She'd fretted less for a date, for Pete's sake.

But she had to walk a fine line. Tanner was not only a customer and a neighbor, but someone Mr. Frank had entrusted her to look after. So, she'd chosen comfortable jeans, a white sleeveless blouse, sandals and her denim floppy hat. Casual, but a step up from shorts and T-shirt with her company logo.

She shifted the stuffed paper bags in her arms and tapped the door with her foot. "Come on, Tanner," she mumbled. "Open the door." On a mission to welcome him to the neighborhood, she also hoped her gifts would make him realize how much she'd loved and respected his grandfather.

Unfortunately, she had another, less pure motive for such a quick return visit: Tanner had filled her thoughts all day.

After she'd left Fairfax House, she had stopped by the office to log in any deliveries and bring home the mail. For the remainder of the afternoon she had helped her crew install light fixtures at a job site. Thank goodness the routine work hadn't required her full attention.

All her life, Cassie had been told she had too much curiosity, so her job proved the perfect fit. She saw hidden treasures in old, beaten-up things. Stripping paint from a piece of furniture to expose the natural beauty underneath was a joy, not a chore.

So, why wouldn't a man such as Tanner, unlike the other men in New Haven, fascinate her? He had more walls built up around him than the mansion he'd inherited, which probably explained why he'd never had a long-term relationship with a woman.

Too bad for him that she lived to tear down walls. But, of course, she had no personal motives. She just had to know him better in order to figure out how to convince him to stay.

She gently kicked at the door again. Still no answer.

Movement in the nearest window caught her attention. The door slowly opened. "Come in. Hurry," Tanner whispered.

"What's wrong?" she asked with forced nonchalance. Curiosity over his odd behavior battled with her unwillingness to appear too eager to see him again. Unfazed by the darkness, she headed for the kitchen. She could find her way around the house blindfolded, had done so many times during games of Blind Man's Bluff with her sister. "You act like you're in hiding."

A dimmed swag light revealed the kitchen table crammed with foil-covered dishes and platters. Her mouth watered at the unmistakable aroma of Mrs. Boone's green bean casserole, Mr. Dunne's barbequed chicken and Miss Eva's cinnamon rolls, along with many other specialties just as familiar.

Cassie made room on the table for the sacks. She tore her glance away from the enticing spread and studied Tanner, only to discover something even more tempting—vulnerability.

"You bet I'm hiding, Cassie. I haven't had a minute's peace since I set foot into this house. People have been coming out of the woodwork in droves. Look at all this." He gestured at the food, then glanced back at her. "I didn't even notice you had the sacks or I would've carried them for you. Sorry. It's just that I'm...I'm..."

"Flustered?" The corners of her mouth involuntarily turned upward. Nothing was more adorable than a flustered male. Adorable? Tanner? She didn't want to go there. "Surely you've been in small towns before. We pride ourselves on friendliness."

"I've worked in hundreds, but never lived in one."

"Hundreds? That's a lot of traveling. What kind of work do you do?" Although she already knew the answer, she wanted Tanner to talk about himself. Something told her that he'd be furious to know an investigator had reported on most aspects of his life.

"Carpentry. And I own a construction company."

When Cassie had first learned of Tanner's chosen field, she had felt an instant kinship with him, sight unseen. Now that she'd met him, so restless, closed off, and full of anger, she knew not to read anything into the fact they both owned their own company and enjoyed working with their hands. He had the most beautiful hands, large and tanned....

She shook her head and forced herself to focus on her plan. If he wanted to be truly happy, Tanner needed to understand the importance of roots and accept his birthright. "Construction must be in the blood. That's how Mr. Frank got his start. Residential, mostly. Then he expanded with businesses related to construction—a hardware store, remodeling and repair. But I guess you already know that."

"I'm strictly commercial." Tanner folded his arms against his chest and his muscles strained against the fabric of his shirt. "I know all I need to know about my grandfather. He was used to getting his own way."

Tanner was bullheaded. Just like his grandfather. "Yes, well, most successful people are. And if you don't know it already, the remodeling business I own belonged to your grandfather until two years ago."

His eyes narrowed. "That's pretty young to buy and think you can run your own business."

"Twenty-three isn't that young when you consider I had worked for your grandfather for nine years before that. My father had left me a little money, so between that and a loan, I was able to offer Mr. Frank a fair price. You can check the papers you got from Mr. Samuels."

"I don't care about any of that." Tanner ran a hand through his thick black hair and paced, his boots pounding against the hardwood floor. "*This* is what I don't get." He gestured at the food. "What do these people want from me?"

Cassie's heart ached from Tanner's dismissal of his grandfather, a man she had grown to love as surely as if he'd been a blood relative. She had to make Tanner see how much his grandfather cursed his own pride and stubbornness that had driven away family, that he had loved Tanner, regretted not being in his life, and had wanted to make up for the mistakes he'd made. "All these people want is to make you feel welcome, show how much they respected your grandfather."

"But why would they care what I think? They don't know me."

"You're a Fairfax. That's all they need to know." She grabbed the chilled gallon of milk, then the eggs, bread, cheeses and coffee from one sack. From the other, she gently removed a small pot of ivy, napkins and other paper products.

Tanner stopped pacing and stared at her as if she'd swapped the denim hat she wore for a bucket. "It's that simple?"

"Yep. And I'm warning you, if you haven't gotten an invitation to dinner from my mother yet, it's coming."

"What do you mean? I've been in town one day."

"Like I said, news travels fast."

"Why would your mother invite me to dinner?"

Cassie smiled patiently. "She went to school with your dad. They were sweethearts once. Later on, Mom took care of your grandmother until she died, and then did the same for your grandfather. They treated Mom, my sister and me like family."

He shook his head and frowned. "I just don't get it."

"You will. Eventually." At least, Cassie hoped that someday soon he'd realize family and roots meant everything. She carried the plant over to the sink and placed the ivy on the window ledge above it.

"Is that some kind of plant? What are you doing?"

"Someone threw out the plants that used to be in here. So, I brought a replacement." She untangled the vines and smiled. Perfect. "The kitchen looks more cozy already."

"Cozy? I don't care about cozy. And I certainly can't take it with me, since I'm never home."

She could almost see the protective walls form around him. "I can't imagine not wanting a place to feel like home, even for a little while." But then, she decorated the inside of her van.

"Look, home is just an apartment where I collect the mail and clean clothes and that's the way I like it."

Cassie guessed that finding himself completely alone at seventeen had shattered any illusions about home and hearth. Although nothing could bring back his parents, she could help him connect to a part of his family he'd never known. But first, he needed to forgive his grandfather.

Boy, did she ever have her work cut out for her. "Fine," she said with a shrug. "I'll take care of the plant for you." She held up a can of coffee. "I didn't know what brand, but guessed you at least wanted caffeine."

"Definitely." His expression even more puzzled,

he approached the table. "How much do I owe you for the groceries?" He pulled his wallet from his back pocket.

She waved away the offer. "If you pay, then I'll have to assume that because my gift isn't homemade it doesn't measure up. I'm not much of a cook or a baker, so I can't compete with all this wonderful food."

"That's not what I meant at all."

"Good." She grinned. "Here's rule number two in a small town—when someone is nice to you, a simple thank you is enough."

She expected some sort of resistance, either a rationalization to pay, or even the return of his earlier wariness. Instead, his dark gaze grew warm, the firm lines of his mouth softened. His expression held something that unnerved her even more—interest.

Tanner snapped out of his flustered fog, jolted by Cassie's lighthearted explanation of why he should put back his wallet. She could have just as easily pouted or acted insulted by his offer of money. How refreshing. He smiled. "Thank you."

Her eyes grew wide, her face flushed. She fidgeted with the denim hat that covered most of her rich brown hair. Not many women pulled off wearing hats, in his opinion, but it looked natural on Cassie.

"You—you're welcome."

In fact, he suspected she'd look good in just about anything. Tonight, instead of overalls, faded jeans outlined dangerous curves. A sleeveless blouse revealed well-defined arms. Bright-pink toenails poked out of sandals, the vivid, feminine color a further reminder that she was all woman.

As if he could forget.

She inched backward toward the kitchen door. "I—I'll see you in the morning, then. Good night," she said, then left.

Tanner walked over to the sink and splashed cold water on his face. He untucked his shirt and used it as a towel, hoping to also wipe away the image now firm in his mind of Cassie's tempting package of curves and muscle, firmness and warmth.

Damn. He wanted to see Cassie as just a hired hand, not a woman. She was too sentimental and emotional. Tears had threatened at the mention of his power-hungry grandfather. She'd reacted to a smile and a thank you the way some women responded to a compliment or flowers.

Yes, he had derived satisfaction from managing to fluster her. And he couldn't deny he was glad, even grateful, to discover that she also felt the chemistry between them. But he'd ignore the attraction. One reason had brought him to New Haven—to inherit the house in order to sell it.

Thirty days and counting. After that, the entire town could swarm Fairfax House. He'd be gone.

Saturday morning at nine o'clock sharp, Cassie knocked on the kitchen door of Fairfax House and braced herself to see Tanner again. She just hoped he wouldn't mention her frazzled state last night, which had been entirely his fault. His unexpected smile had softened his features and reminded her of how moments earlier she'd found him adorable. Then he'd given her *that look*.

Once home and in her own bed, she'd tossed and turned for hours. Had she imagined the curiosity in his gaze? If her instincts were correct, would any interest on his part prove a complication or an asset in her attempt to convince him to remain at Fairfax House?

No. The tantalizing notion wouldn't get another thought. Besides just being plain wrong to capitalize on whatever chemistry existed between them, she'd never been one to do things the easy way.

The aroma of strong coffee and cinnamon streamed through the screen door and made serious thinking difficult. Her mouth watered, her stomach grumbled, and she silently cursed her weakness for sweets. She didn't need any distractions.

She wanted something from Tanner Fairfax, something she could almost taste, the way she could already taste the perfect blend of cinnamon and sugars in Miss Eva's famous rolls. She didn't care if Tanner acted bitter, suspicious, flustered or even flirty. She'd deal with whatever he threw at her.

"Come in." He held the door open.

"Thanks." She stepped inside. Her determination to act naturally took a nosedive at the sight of Tanner, obviously fresh out of the shower. Drops of water clung to his hair. A navy T-shirt outlined his broad chest. Gray gym shorts revealed tanned, lean, muscular legs.

So, her customer was attractive. Not a problem.

She swallowed hard and forced her thoughts back to business. "Before I forget, another customer still has my wallpaper books. I can have them here in a day or so, if that's okay."

"Sure." The door banged shut as he walked across the kitchen, his weathered sneakers silent on the tiled floor. "How about coffee and a roll before you start? This good food shouldn't go to waste."

He nodded at two places already set with paper plates and napkins at the kitchen table.

She didn't know what to make of his almost formal manner, the polite smile. Not a smidgen of curiosity. Apparently, she'd tossed and turned for no reason last night.

She was okay with that, though. Polite, she could handle. "Only a fool would turn down that offer." She took a seat, determined to keep things light, friendly, but still professional, in order to win his trust.

"Butter?" he asked.

With a guilty start she shook her head and turned her thoughts to the safer topic of breakfast. She unwound a portion of the roll coated with homemade icing, tore off a piece and popped it in her mouth.

"Heaven," she murmured, savoring the sinfully rich confection, heavy on the cinnamon and some other blend of spices which remained Miss Eva's secret. Bit by bit, she unraveled the roll, enjoying each delicious bite.

She glanced up to find Tanner staring at her. "What's wrong? Do I have a frosting mustache or something?"

"No," he answered quickly. "Nothing like that. I mean, I've never seen anyone eat a roll like that before."

"When something is this good, I try to make it last even longer. Don't worry, though. With wallpapering, I charge by the roll, not the hour." She wiped her fingers on the napkin next to her plate. Teetering on the edge of sugar overload, she took a sip of coffee as strong as the aroma had promised.

Over the rim of her cup she caught him studying

her as if she were a complex blueprint. What had she said or done?

"I'm not worried." He nudged his plate away, having already inhaled two buttered rolls before she'd finished one. Obviously, he didn't share her tendency to savor. "I didn't mean to rush you," he continued, "you were on time this morning, which is refreshing in itself."

"I can't take credit for that. I live across the street in Mrs. Boone's upstairs apartment."

He chuckled and leaned back in his chair. "Seems like I was recently told that when someone says something nice to you, a simple thank you is enough."

She smiled, surprised and much too pleased by his sudden shift from impersonal politeness to friendly bantering. "A quick study. I like that. And you got points last night for not commenting on the fact that I don't cook or bake."

"Big deal. I've never spent any time in a kitchen, either."

"But my mom and sister put Martha Stewart to shame."

"That bad, huh?"

"Worse." She much preferred this relaxed version of Tanner over the guarded one, for the sake of keeping her promise to Mr. Frank, of course. She had to earn Tanner's trust. "Have you checked out the barn yet?"

"It was locked. I'll call the lawyer about a key."

"A spare key is in the broom closet. You'll love the barn, Tanner. There's so much history in it. Right now, it's just storage for your grandfather's old Thunderbird, but when your great-grandfather lived here, this house was actually out in the country and he traded horses. The town spread out until Fairfax House ended up in the middle of town. You're allowed to keep the barn because it's the original structure.''

Her cellular phone rang. ''Excuse me, Tanner.'' Cassie dug the phone out of a bib pocket and checked the phone number. Good. ''It's my painter. I'll just be a minute.'' She put the phone up to her ear. ''Hey, Georgie.''

''Hi, Cas. I'm on my way to Mr. Dibble's place. And I wanted to thank you again for letting me off early yesterday. Emily scored the team's only goal!''

Cassie grinned as she pictured the curly-haired six-year-old in her purple-and-white uniform. ''Not a problem, Georgie. Looks like I owe her an ice-cream cone.''

''Now, Cas, it isn't necessary to bribe. She lives to tear up the field.''

''I know. But she's so cute, I'd end up treating her anyway. Oh, and in case you forgot, wait a while after you ring Mr. Dibble's doorbell. He uses a walker and might take a while to get to the door. And don't waste much time going over paint chips. He always ends up choosing the original color.''

''Okay. I'll check in later, then. Bye.''

''Bye.'' Cassie hung up and dropped the phone into a pocket, aware that she didn't have any time to waste, either. She had less than a month to make Tanner feel connected to Fairfax House, to New Haven.

''Is your business a family operation?'' Tanner's deep voice interrupted her thoughts.

''No. There's only me. But I'm all for the idea. I

think a family that works together, stays together."
She had observed too many couples drift apart while
chasing after different dreams; her sister was a perfect example.

Tanner looked as if he'd taken a bite of lemon.
No surprise there.

"Why do you ask?" she persisted.

He shrugged. "I just assumed. Why else would
you know if a worker is hurting for money, or if their
kid has a game?"

Cassie smiled. Questions, the first sign of interest.
"That's the beauty of small-town life. It's second
nature to me, since I've either grown up with or
around these people. I always prefer to use local subcontractors, people I can trust." When she cared, remembering the important things was easy. "I take it
things are a little different where you come from?"

"You could say that."

Darn. A closed door. Somehow, she needed to
spark Tanner's interest in the house, in his family
history. Maybe she should start with what fascinated
her the most about the mansion. "This may sound
crazy, but I have a favor to ask."

Tanner raised his eyebrows. "A favor?"

She rarely allowed distractions during work, but
she had more than one job to do. The price and the
time frame for the repairs to the kitchen had already
been agreed upon. Her other job, her promise to do
all she could to convince Tanner to make Fairfax
House his home, was a freebie, no invoice required.
"Would you mind if I went upstairs for a look-see?"

"Do you suspect more water damage?"

"No. The damage was limited to the separate roof
above the kitchen. This is sort of personal." She

leaned forward, elbows on the table. "I've been in this house many times, but my sister and I were never allowed to go upstairs. It seems silly, I know, but the spiral staircase always reminded me of a beanstalk."

She paused and grinned. "I desperately wanted to be like Jack and climb that sucker. Later, when I got closer to Mr. Frank, it seemed too much of an invasion of privacy to ask. Not to mention sort of odd. But I've always wondered what was so special or scary about the upstairs that kept it out of bounds."

"But you've been working in this house. If it was that big of a deal, why didn't you just look on your own?"

"I was tempted. But it felt disrespectful."

"Some willpower."

"Tell me about it. But now that you're the owner, I won't feel guilty if you say it's okay."

Tanner unfolded his long frame. Dark eyes shined with amusement. "Lead the way."

"Great." She hurried through the parlor and formal living room to the ornate staircase, breathless with anticipation. The last time she recalled feeling this excited was as a child on Christmas morning. Well, maybe as an adult last Christmas. She hadn't changed that much. The fact that Tanner followed closely behind only added to her eagerness.

Maybe she could hook his interest with one of her favorite stories. "This staircase originally came down into the dining room. Your grandmother mentioned how much better it would look this way, and the next day Mr. Frank brought in an architect. He would've done just about anything for her." Anything except admit he'd been wrong about what mattered to her most—their son.

Cassie paused at the bottom step. The stairs seemed to have shrunk over the past twenty years, but what lay beyond was huge and she felt daunted by the immense responsibility before her. She had learned not to take promises lightly; she would not let Mr. Frank down.

"Go on." Tanner urged. "But don't get your hopes up. I did a quick inspection last night—I was too beat from driving straight through to do more. It's just hallways and rooms."

Cassie refused to buy into his pessimism. Although she had asked to explore as a ruse to snare Tanner's interest in his family, she was still excited to finally have the chance to appease her curiosity.

She slowly made her way up the wooden steps, trailing her hand along the smooth banister. She'd waited a long time for this opportunity and wanted to savor every moment. "I'll bet Mr. Frank is smiling right now. He always warned me that I had an overactive imagination."

"I don't get it, Cassie. Once you got older, what made you want to hang around an old guy you weren't even related to?"

Her plan had worked! More questions, the first step toward understanding. "My father died when I was nine. My mom and sister found comfort in doing things together. Cooking, baking, sewing. Things I was dreadful at. That's why I enjoyed puttering around with my dad in the yard and garage so much." Having lost that connection, she'd never felt so alone in her life. And guilty.

Just before her father passed away, he'd asked her

to promise to be less of a tomboy. Her mother didn't need more to worry about, and she fretted that Cassie would never fit in. Once he was gone, they would all need to lean on one another.

Cassie had tried to act more like her sister, a girlie-girl, but it proved such a bad fit, she'd given up. So much for keeping promises. "Your grandfather, bless his heart, saw how lost I was and found things for me to do around this house."

She realized, looking back, that the old man had been just as lost as that frightened young girl. Before long, she even thought of the house as a lost soul—locked in dark colors and heavy wood, unhappiness and regret in every corner.

Such a treasure deserved a second chance. If Tanner decided to put down roots in New Haven he could bring the house into the light, turn it into a home, not just a pristine, cold showcase.

More importantly, though, Tanner would have found where he truly belonged. He'd lost so much already. "Let's see what's behind door number one." Cassie opened the door and strolled inside the room, surprised to find she had been holding her breath.

Darn. Just peach-colored walls, elegant furniture and a lingering scent of mothballs.

Tanner followed Cassie inside the room. He pictured her, lonely and missing her dad, racing off to do repairs in the old house, and felt a sharp tug on his heart.

He knew how working with your hands could soothe your soul. After he'd lost his parents in a car wreck when he was seventeen, a nonprofit group called Mentors, Inc. had hooked him up with a master carpenter who specialized in framing and building cabinets on-site.

Tanner had thrown himself into the part-time job to curb his loneliness. Wood was solid, yet he could coax it to his will. *He* determined the shape, texture, even the color. Control of any kind had worked like a bandage against the open sore of helplessness that had raged inside of him.

He doubted he'd have to explain to Cassie how that job had become a lifeline to an angry, scared kid in search of direction and purpose.

At least he'd been old enough to declare himself emancipated, and could make his own decisions about his future. He had stayed with neighbors, who were also close friends to his parents, until he graduated from high school and got his own apartment.

Man, he hadn't thought about those dark times in ages. Didn't care to, either. He'd rather contemplate the fascinating woman next to him who was real, unpretentious and obviously unaware of her effect on him.

Who was he kidding? She probably had the same effect on all men, was probably involved with someone. No. He wouldn't think about her personal life; it was none of his business.

"The antiques are so beautiful." Cassie's soft voice pulled him back to the present. "Too bad they can't talk. I'll bet they have wonderful stories." She slowly ran her hand along the curved back of a cherry rocker.

She hadn't simply touched the chair, she'd caressed it. He marveled at how she milked the simplest of pleasures for all they were worth.

At breakfast, observing her lost in the taste, smell

and feel of the pastry had thrown him off balance. In no time, his cool politeness had been replaced with a keen awareness of the sensual woman across the table. He'd found himself relaxing, had even razzed her about a simple thank you after she'd shrugged off his compliment for promptness.

Minutes later he had agreed to explore the upstairs with her. The spontaneous act had felt natural, which amazed him, since he'd denied that part of himself for so many years. He had learned quickly that spontaneity was for other people, not for someone like him who had lost his parents, his anchors, much too early in his life.

Cassie's slow ascent up the staircase she'd been dying to climb for years had impressed him, made him wonder if she would approach lovemaking with the same drawn-out passion....

Tanner nearly groaned at the thought. In less than a month he'd return to Texas. He had no business thinking of her in that way. Damn. He needed a distraction. "What do you think this room was used for?" he asked as he opened the doors of an intricately carved armoire.

"It might have been your dad's, if that picture means anything." She walked over to the nightstand, picked up an ornate silver picture frame and offered it to him. "Do you recognize anyone, Tanner?"

He wanted to walk away, but couldn't. Cassie placed the frame in his hands, the heavy metal cool to the touch.

He traced the outline of a young boy with familiar dark hair and eyes sitting on the back of a red convertible, no doubt the Thunderbird Cassie had mentioned earlier. An obviously proud father stood off to the side.

"They look happy in that picture, don't they?"

Tanner returned the frame to Cassie, determined not to show a reaction to the photograph. No way did he want to imagine his grandfather as a typical, doting dad. He was a monster who had hassled his family. "Nice car."

She gazed at him expectantly, but he had nothing to say that she'd want to hear. "Let's check the next room," she finally said.

Up and down the hallway, her enthusiasm built with each step. Her excitement proved contagious. Tanner followed, grateful for a distraction. How could someone so curious possess the willpower not to sneak upstairs on one of her many visits? Despite himself, he was impressed.

She hurried to the next room. "Jill is going to gloat. She never believed there was anything special up here."

"Jill. That's your sister, right?"

"Right. The one without an imagination." Cassie stopped in front of the last room. "What made you choose this room, Tanner?"

He blinked. "Choose it for what?"

"Your room. None of your stuff was in the other rooms, and this is the only one left."

"I tossed my dufflebag in the room downstairs."

She raised an eyebrow. "In case you didn't notice, the bed downstairs is a double. All the beds that we've seen up here are queen or king-size. But hey, whatever floats your boat."

She turned her attention to the next room. "I sure

hope this one is more interesting.'' She opened the door and stepped inside.

Tanner followed close behind. "More interesting, maybe, but nothing exciting." Heavy, stale air assaulted him. Light poured in from high windows and revealed a long, narrow room that ran the length of the house. The perfect space for storage.

"Wow," Cassie murmured. "Looks like a Hitchcock movie set."

"The only things missing are a few rabid birds." A sloped ceiling created a tunnel affect. At one end stood an enormous oak rolltop desk and shelves that sagged under the weight of too many books. The opposite side of the room held an armoire and several trunks. Cobwebs cloaked every surface.

"Just look at that Victrola, Tanner! I can almost hear big-band music and picture giggling teenage girls teaching one another the latest dance steps."

He watched Cassie rush across a massive, faded, Oriental rug to the Victrola.

"I knew it! Jill and I would've had a blast in here. And of course, probably destroyed every breakable thing in sight." She took a rag from a back pocket and flicked it across the lid of the antique, destroying at least one spider's home while she whipped up a miniature dust storm.

She sneezed and waved her hand to clear the air, a grin on her face all the while. A blanket of dust and a maze of sticky cobwebs failed to dim her excitement. The sparkle in her eyes made him want to keep giving her reasons to be excited. A dangerous thought. He planned to leave as soon as possible so there wouldn't be time to...to what? Build a relationship?

Not an option.

Once again he needed a diversion and stopped at the first thing in front of him, a fancy table with a glass case on top. Four rows of tarnished spoons nestled against faded black velvet.

"Tanner, look. I found some old letters addressed to your grandmother. What did you find?" Cassie approached him and gasped. "These collectibles are from all over the world. You should get a safety deposit box."

Vivid childhood memories popped into his mind. His truck-driving father had always brought back a souvenir spoon from each town he visited as a gift for his mother. They had explained how the spoons symbolized their freedom. The real collection and more could've been theirs if they had agreed to let his grandfather run their lives. He had insisted they return to New Haven, or send Tanner to live with him in order to benefit from the opportunities money and status provided. Of course they had refused.

Tanner had thought it silly how happy the cheap gifts had made his mother. Now, as he gazed at the impressive collection, he understood why she had claimed that a spoon from Peoria was more valuable than a collectible from Paris.

His throat tightened. A strange wetness appeared behind his eyes at the reminder of how much pain his grandfather had caused his parents. He was more convinced than ever that he'd done the right thing by coming to New Haven. Finally, he could make good on the promise he'd made to his parents while he knelt at their graves so long ago. Delayed justice, but sweet just the same.

He didn't need the money, only the satisfaction he'd feel when he sold the very thing his grandfather had valued over family.

"Tanner? What's wrong?"

Chapter Three

"**Y**ou can keep the letters if you want or toss them. I don't care. I'm done exploring." Tanner walked out of the storage room and down the stairs, away from Cassie's concerned, questioning gaze.

Damn. He should never have let the collection get to him.

He roamed from the dining room to the parlor and pulled out drawers of an old desk. He made an attempt to inspect the contents, but instead he saw Cassie's face, how the sparkle in her eyes had vanished after his curt words in the storage room.

So what? Her fun had been cut short. She'd live.

In the meantime, he'd just stay away from Cassie, who had probably returned to work by now. She didn't need his help, and he was still embarrassed that he'd allowed her to see his reaction to the spoons.

Whimsical humming drifted from the kitchen. The gentle reminder he wasn't alone brought back warm memories of his mother. The kitchen had been his favorite room in the compact house he'd grown up in. He had even done his homework at the table, for the snacks and drinks, or so he had told his mother. A teenage boy would never admit how he'd found comfort in her nearness as she hummed and flitted about the tiny room.

Without fussing over him, she had always seemed to know what he wanted and needed. He had felt safe and loved. When his grandfather had stepped up his campaign to lure him to New Haven, Tanner had never wavered, confident of where he belonged and who he could depend on to always be there for him.

But that was a long time ago. He had learned the hard way not to let someone get close to him; the pain was gut-wrenching when they left.

He had coped with the loss of his parents; he had made something of his life. What he had to deal with now, a live-in clause, was simply an irritation.

Too distracted to continue his search, he plopped down on the carpet, hooked his feet under the Queen Anne sofa and did sit-ups. Minutes later he stopped, restless and bored.

He had no idea what to do next—a rare problem. The construction business provided endless challenges, from high turnover of employees to the ever changing weather. He preferred work outdoors and stomping out figurative fires over some caged-in desk job.

Fanciful humming continued from the kitchen, and he followed, unsure why, except that idleness was pure torture and he'd have to face Cassie some time.

He reached the kitchen and opened the door to the

familiar scent of vanilla. She must go through that stuff by the case.

Cassie had her back to him and was meticulously peeling away the old wallpaper. Without warning, he pictured the room with new paper, fresh paint and plants everywhere. In his mind, Cassie sat at the table with a small, dark-haired boy with blue eyes on her lap.

The scene screamed "home." Family. Things he'd never allowed himself to want.

Life was too uncertain to get attached to things, places, people. He dated, sure, but only women who shared his philosophy of no strings. He didn't want marriage, let alone a family. He'd barely survived the loss of his parents. The thought of losing a wife or child, whether through death or even divorce, chilled him to the bone, making the decision to remain unattached the only choice he could live with.

He shook his head to clear the unsettling images. Nothing and no one would make him care about Fairfax House, his vengeful grandfather, or make him want the very things that could destroy him. "Can I help with anything in here?" he finally said, in need of some logical reason for bothering her.

Cassie turned, a surprised expression on her face. "Excuse me?"

"I'm not good at sitting around doing nothing."

"Something is bothering you, Tanner. It might help to talk."

"It'll help more if I just make myself useful."

She tilted her head, as if studying him. "There is something, then. I'd like to run ideas by you about different paper and paint for in here before you look at the sample books. I'm thinking white paint on the woodwork. Now, I know most men, and carpenters in particular, prefer stain, and I usually do, too, but all this wood makes the room too dark and uninviting.''

At least she hadn't mentioned the blasted spoon collection. ''I might have an opinion if I was going to live here. Do whatever you think will get this place sold the quickest.''

She winced. ''You know that your grandfather hoped you would make this house your home. His letter... Wait a minute. I'll bet you haven't even read it, have you?''

Tanner did a double take. ''How did you know about that?''

''I was with him when he wrote it. He desperately wanted to see you, to apologize, and ask for your forgiveness. So, he wrote the letter and I mailed it for him. Please, read it before you make any decisions about the house.''

No rationale or apology could make up for the pain his grandfather had caused. ''Not interested.''

''So, you won't even consider keeping the house?''

Keep it? If he could've attained justice any other way, he would never have set foot inside Fairfax House. ''You can't know the whole story, or you wouldn't even ask that question.''

''He told me everything, Tanner. How he disowned your dad for marrying your mom, pregnant with you. That from the time you were five until your parents died, he made threats and offered bribes to get you to come live with him. And even though your grandmother begged him to make amends, he refused.''

The abbreviated list of the old man's manipulations renewed Tanner's resentment and left him with more than a bad taste in his mouth, but he'd get over it, just as he'd gotten over every other setback life had thrown at him. He pushed the negative thoughts aside, refused to let his grandfather cause him another moment of suffering. "Then it should be clear why I'm selling."

"No, it's not. I know you're angry with your grandfather, and you have every right, but I swear to you, he had changed and wanted to make amends. Did you ever stop to think how you'll feel when you finally accept the truth about your grandfather? Will you be able to forgive yourself for being too proud to accept his apology and make peace with the past before he died? If you sell this house, your birthright, you'll feel even worse."

"Don't waste your time worrying about me. In fact, why do you even care? This has nothing to do with you."

"It does, in a way. I went through something similar to what you're going through when my dad died. We had a fight a few days before, we weren't even speaking, and the next thing I knew he was dead. At first I felt guilty, thinking it was my fault he had died. Then I got angry at him for dying and leaving me. Finally, I hated myself for not making up right away. It was a long time before I could forgive myself. But once I did, there was a tremendous sense of peace. And I—"

Tanner shook his head. "You were what, nine? And I'm guessing your dad, for the most part, was a good guy. Our situations are nothing alike."

"Okay, forget about all that. What about your

grandmother? She never did anything to hurt you. What about your father? He grew up in this house, this town. There's a sense of history and roots. Generations of Fairfaxes have lived and died in New Haven.''

''My parents, the only family I cared about, lived and died in Tyler, Texas. If it wasn't for the live-in clause I'd sell to the highest bidder today. The lawyer told me there's interest.''

She blinked. ''Of course there's interest. It's prime real estate. But, you can't be serious.''

He didn't owe the old man anything, but he owed his parents plenty and would make his grandfather pay for his selfishness. ''Try me.''

She frowned, looked away and turned her attention back to her work.

''If you're that concerned, why don't *you* bid on the house?''

Startled green eyes met his. ''I just might.''

The determination in her voice convinced him that she wasn't bluffing. He couldn't imagine why a piece of property meant so much to her. A place she'd only visited, with no ties to her own family. ''What's so special about this house?''

''This isn't just any house, Tanner. It's where your great-grandmother threw her famous parties for New Haven's high society. Where Mr. Frank moved an entire staircase to please your grandmother.''

She pointed to the ceiling. ''On this kitchen roof is where your dad jumped off on a dare and broke his arm. In the parlor there's a trunk full of yellowed drawing paper, crayons and Pick-Up Sticks that I used to play with when I came along with my mom when I was a little girl. They probably belonged to your dad. This house has memories, memories that shouldn't be forgotten.''

Tanner disagreed. In the time it took to pound a nail into wood, your whole life could change. One morning he'd been a senior in high school whose biggest worry was if he'd made first string on the football team. Then the two people he cared about most in the world had been ripped away from him. ''You can live in the past, but I prefer the present. If you make your offer competitive, the house will be yours. But before it can be sold, a lot of work needs to be done. What can I do to help?''

She opened her mouth as if to speak, but instead she shook her head. ''It wouldn't be right. I've been paid to do this work.''

He'd never fought so hard for permission to work for no pay. ''I won't tell if you won't.''

''I'm real particular. Just ask my crew.'' She grimaced. ''Better yet, don't.''

''If you have a crew, why are you doing the grunt work?''

''My subcontractors are busy on other job sites. Besides, I promised your grandfather I'd take care of this personally.''

Tanner wondered again about Cassie's motives. Had she been promised something by his grandfather to make it worth her while to help his cause? The lawyer might have some answers.

He watched Cassie study him, obviously still struggling with her decision on whether or not to put him to work. ''Have you painted before?''

Tanner preferred to work with wood in its raw form. He enjoyed the process of measuring and cutting in order to create something from nothing. He had an experienced crew that handled the stain and paint, but he'd observed enough to know the basics. "Not specifically. But I'm good with my hands and a quick study. How much damage can I do under your supervision?"

She hesitated.

"Look at it this way, Cassie. I'm the closest thing to an owner now, right? So if I screw up it's my problem."

"I guess you are the boss," she finally said, but without enthusiasm.

Not the greatest vote of approval, but he'd take it.

"It's against my better judgment, but if you insist, you can prime all the wood in this room. It's already been sanded. Are you sure that you're okay with white cabinets?"

"Whatever. Although you must've been pretty confident of my answer if you already have the supplies here."

"I'd say more optimistic than confident."

She spread out a drop cloth and gave a crash course on painting. "And don't bloat the brush with too much primer."

He performed a few practice strokes and she nodded with approval. "Tanner, are you sure you want to do this?"

"Positive."

"Okay, but don't hesitate to ask questions or stop all together if you don't feel like doing it anymore. Deal?"

"Deal."

She returned to her wallpaper stripping, but with obvious reluctance. Not that he blamed her, though.

He tended to hover over job sites. In her place, he doubted that he would've been so generous.

Painting proved more of a challenge than he anticipated. He ignored the fumes and eagerly lost himself in the process. With each stroke, he brushed away painful memories.

"Um, Tanner, I appreciate your wanting to help," Cassie said from behind his shoulder. Annoyed at the interruption, he turned to face her. "But I just don't feel right about this," she continued. "I'm sure you have more important things to do, people to see, questions about your grandfather's estate."

"I have questions, all right," he said, irritated at being yanked back to reality. The questions churned in his mind. How could a monster like his grandfather have any blood ties to a man as good, generous and loving as his father? What kind of man punished his son for marrying the mother of his child?

Tanner grimly placed the brush on the rim of the can, then paused at the sight of his white hands.

His gaze flew to his work area and he groaned. More primer covered the drop cloth and his clothes than the paneling. "I guess I'm not much of a painter." He stared at his hands, so capable with a hammer and a screwdriver. How could they be so pitiful with a lousy paintbrush? "It looks so easy. Sorry. I'll help clean up."

"It's not a problem. Really. I'm sure you'd get the hang of it after a while."

The kindness in her voice amazed Tanner. If she was as particular as she had claimed, she must be irritated, even angry over the mess he'd made and the wasted primer.

And he'd obviously upset her earlier with talk of

selling to the highest bidder, even though it was the truth. Still, he could've been less of a jerk and not taken his resentment toward his grandfather out on her.

Why didn't she just yell at him? He'd feel better.

Cassie observed Tanner as he inspected his paint-splattered hands. His expression was a mixture of surprise and confusion, as if his hands had betrayed him somehow. Her irritation over his threat to wage a bidding war over Fairfax House had already begun to fade. She'd known that was just bitterness toward his grandfather talking and had nothing to do with her.

A part of her admired his loyalty to his parents. Once he cared, once he gave his word, he'd never back down. But that same stubbornness was responsible for why he couldn't forgive.

She had agreed to let Tanner paint for one reason—she had hoped that if he personally worked on the house, he'd develop a vested interest, maybe even a sense of ownership. Time would tell, but he'd have to find some other way to "help." He was a lousy painter.

As for the wasted primer, sure, she'd have to replace it, but that only required a trip to the store. Somehow she doubted such a simple solution existed for whatever bothered Tanner.

"Here. Use this." Cassie offered Tanner a rag soaked in paint thinner. He swiped roughly at his hands then absently returned the damp cloth, his callused fingers brushing against hers.

She couldn't move.

A palpable energy radiated from him, sucked the air from the room, from her lungs and left her weak-kneed. She hadn't felt such a jolt since she was five years old and had poked a bobby pin in a light socket. But instead of pain, this experience was charged with fear and excitement.

She tried to blame her sudden unbalance on the paint thinner fumes, but knew she'd grown accustomed to that odor years ago.

Tanner's startled gaze flew to her face, searching, as if seeing her for the first time. As if he found her baggy uniform sexy and preferred her natural look over a made-up one. As if he actually liked what he saw.

No doubt about it, he was aware of her as a woman.

A part of her wanted to run for safety, while the curious side of her yearned to discover what would happen if their touches weren't accidental, if their lips were to touch, if…

No. She shook her head to clear the crazy thoughts. No matter how incredible the chemistry, she wouldn't risk personal involvement. If she failed to keep her promise, and Tanner sold the house and left town, she had no intention of letting him take her heart as well.

Tanner blinked, as if coming out of a trance. He shoved his hands in his pockets and took an awkward step backward. "I've done enough damage in here. I think I'll check out the barn."

Relief swept over Cassie, since the only real damage he'd done was to her equilibrium. To make matters worse, his reaction just now proved she wasn't the only one affected by innocent physical contact. "Good idea." She fetched the key from the broom closet. "You'll need this to get in," she said, grateful he seemed as willing as she was to ignore the chemistry between them.

He stared at the closet, at the key held between his long fingers, then frowned. "Thanks," he mumbled, and disappeared through the kitchen door.

"No—thank you," she said softly, grateful he had gone. The man changed moods quicker than she could talk herself out of wearing a dress; he was obviously struggling with something.

He'd momentarily let his guard down and teased her, joined her in a treasure hunt, then knocked her for another loop with a high-voltage touch, only to slip back into grim aloofness.

She was beginning to think Tanner needed a makeover as much as the house.

Tanner barreled out of the kitchen to the side porch, relieved to have put distance between himself and the unsettling woman inside. Within seconds his shirt had become sticky against his back and chest, but he refused to return indoors to the cool air-conditioning.

He took a deep breath and inhaled the scent of promised rain that hung in the midday air. The encouraging fact failed to hold his attention. It might rain. Big deal.

All he could think about was the incredible sparks that had just resulted from brushing his fingers against Cassie's. She'd gotten under his skin, which caused him more discomfort than Ohio's humidity. He'd sweat bullets before he'd face her any time soon.

What would happen if they ever kissed?

No. He didn't need such a complication in his life. One reason only had brought him to New Haven—

to serve the stipulated time in order to sell the house and make good on his promise to his parents.

He didn't want to hear kind words about a manipulative grandfather, could care less about making friends, and a fling that might create ties remained out of the question.

He needed to keep resisting Cassie...but how, when he couldn't seem to say no to her, from what color of paint to use to granting her request to explore the upstairs? He preferred the comfort of predictability and didn't want spontaneity back in his life.

Nothing about his reaction to Cassie was logical, especially why the fact she was so at home in Fairfax House had bothered him. She'd known where to find a broom to clean up her mess, as well as the key to the barn. The history of the house and his family tumbled from her inviting lips. He didn't regret turning down every opportunity to live in the house with his grandparents, so it shouldn't matter if someone else had taken his place. But it did bother him. And he had no idea why.

A black Lexus pulled up to the curb and Mr. Samuels, the lawyer he'd met with yesterday, exited. Tall, reed-thin and white-haired, the elderly man appeared as if a strong wind could blow him over.

"Good afternoon, Mr. Fairfax."

"It's Tanner. Is there a problem?" Tanner asked, suddenly alert. He had planned to contact the lawyer anyway, so the visit saved him a phone call, but the unexpected appearance made Tanner more suspicious than grateful.

"No, no, nothing like that." The lawyer leaned

forward, his expression concerned. "Have you had some sort of accident?"

Confused, Tanner glanced down to find white splatters all over his shirt and shorts. "No. It's a long story. "

"I see. I take it, then, that Miss Leighton is doing a good job on the repairs?"

"Sure." Although she had done an even better job of keeping him off balance. "What did you need to see me about?"

"Actually, I'm here to ask a favor."

Tanner wondered if he had *pushover* splashed all over him in addition to paint. First, Cassie and her favors to explore and paint cabinets, and now the lawyer. "What kind of favor?"

"Next month is our town's Founder's Day festival. Since a Fairfax helped build this town, we've always had someone in the family lead the parade in Frank's Thunderbird. Would you do the honors this year?"

Tanner blinked. "Me?"

"Of course. You're a Fairfax. The town council had an emergency meeting last night and the vote was unanimous."

The whole town was nuts to blindly accept a stranger. "Sorry. Parades aren't my thing. But I did have some questions. Can you arrange an estate sale as soon as possible?"

Disappointment etched the old man's face. "Of course, but you must satisfy the conditions of the will first, or the estate and its contents will go to the Historical Society."

"That won't happen." The last thing Tanner

wanted was for the house to be turned into a shrine to his grandfather.

"Regardless, nothing official can be done for thirty days, which happens to fall on the first day of the festival. The entire town gets in on the festivities. It would actually hurt your chances for a good turn-out and the best prices to schedule your sale too close to the festival."

"Do I have to be here for the actual sale?"

"No. In fact, many people prefer not to be present. It's too painful to watch their family possessions being bought."

Tanner smothered the urge to laugh. He'd like nothing better than to witness what his grandfather valued most being auctioned off to strangers. But, he planned to give the money from the sale to Mentors, Inc., and he wouldn't cheat them out of the best prices. If he hadn't been paired up with a master carpenter after his parents died he might have ended up in a gutter somewhere or worse. Other kids deserved a similar lifeline to grab on to when they needed help the most.

"Arrange the sale for when you think is best, but I don't want this to drag on. And keep in mind, it's no longer thirty days, but twenty-nine, and counting. I'll be putting up a For Sale sign on Monday."

"And you're certain you don't want to use a Realtor?"

"It's pretty straightforward. I think I can handle it."

"Yes, well, I'll see what I can set up in regard to the estate sale. As for the other matter, could we at least have your permission to use your grandfather's Thunderbird in the parade? It would mean a lot to the town. Frank, Sr. was highly respected in the community.''

Probably bought his way into respectability. ''Makes no difference to me.'' Tanner ignored the twinge of curiosity over the car. He used to work on classics for a second job whenever commercial building slowed down in Tyler.

''We would pay to have it serviced beforehand, of course.''

For a moment, Tanner was tempted to offer tuning up the car himself, since idleness put him on edge. How else would he fill the time? Cassie wouldn't let him near a brush and paint anytime soon. He'd figure something out. He shrugged. ''Whatever.''

''I guess you didn't inherit your dad and grandfather's love of working on cars. I can't tell you how many times I'd drive past this house and see the two of them with their heads under the raised hood.''

Tanner swallowed his surprise. He remembered tinkering on the family truck with his father, both of them covered in grease and sweat and loving every minute. Although Tanner hadn't realized it at the time, his father had taught him life's lessons right along with the explanation of how an engine worked.

Surprise, skepticism and an illogical jealousy thrashed around inside Tanner. He never dreamed that anything he'd shared with his father could have a connection to his grandfather.

''Why your grandfather used to brag—''

''Sorry for interrupting, Mr. Samuels, but I'm in the middle of something right now, and have a few more questions to ask before I get back to it.''

''Yes, of course. What can I do for you?''

''Do I have all the paperwork regarding the estate,

and do you know if my grandfather made any bequests before he died?''

The lawyer frowned. ''What are you implying, young man?''

''Nothing at all, Mr. Samuels.'' Tanner wanted the lawyer on his side. ''Like any smart businessman, I just want to make sure I have all the facts and information.''

''You sounded just like your granddaddy just then,'' the lawyer said, his frown now a sad smile.

Tanner knew the lawyer had meant the comparison as a compliment, but the idea that he shared any of his grandfather's traits made Tanner sick to his stomach.

''I assure you, Tanner, that everything about the estate is in order. As for what he did with any money before he died, he had a right to do whatever he pleased.''

Tanner nodded. ''Well, it's pretty clear that Cassie was close to my grandfather. I imagine he was generous toward her?''

''Frank would've given her something if she would've accepted. The Leightons are proud people, though. Why, Frank tried to give his remodeling business to Cassie and she flat-out refused. Insisted on paying a fair price. I do know for a fact, though, that several local charities received donations. Anything else?''

''Not at the moment. But I want to make sure you understand that I'm not driving the car in the parade.''

''Yes, but if you change your mind, even at the last minute, we'd love to have you. I'll be calling to let you know when someone will be by to pick up the car, and with details on the estate sale.''

"The sooner, the better.''

The old man nodded, shook Tanner's hand and strolled back to his car.

Without a backward glance Tanner headed for the barn, shaking his head. No way was he going to let some town reel him in and try to make him one of their own.

He heard the Lexus start up and drive away. The sun disappeared behind dark clouds. Fat raindrops fell from the sky. Quickening his pace, he reached the barn before the rain had a chance to drench him.

The key turned easily in the padlock. He leaned his weight into the huge wooden sliding door and pushed it all the way open. Dirt and dust stirred at his feet. The smell of straw and leather permeated the thick air.

The car, parked in the center of the barn, was cloaked in a tan custom cover. Chrome wheels peeked out from underneath. He lifted a corner of the tarp and carefully peeled it back a little at a time. His anticipation increased with every revealed, flame-red inch, similar to the thrill of slowly undressing a beautiful woman. So what if he knew what to expect? Each time proved exciting.

He draped the cover over a rail and lowered the soft top, his favorite look on the classic model. The '57 Thunderbird, with its sexy red-and-white interior, seemed out of place amid the dusty tack and worn saddles. He walked around the car to inspect its condition.

He whistled. What a beauty. How fitting to discover his grandfather had taken better care of his car than his family.

Family. The thought reminded him of the picture of his dad he'd seen earlier while exploring the upstairs with Cassie.

Tanner leaned over to touch the top of the back seat where his dad, who must've been about seven, had posed for the picture. So much history, so many intimate family details, gone, because of one man's need to dominate and control.

"Quit feeling sorry for yourself," he muttered out loud as he walked to the front. He raised the hood and found the car as spotless inside as out.

The garage he'd worked in years ago had focused mainly on cars made before computers had come onboard, back when just about anyone could change the oil. He was more than capable of doing a minor tune-up on this baby.

He reached inside to inspect the fluid levels and belts and tried to block out the fact his father and grandfather had worked on this very car, together.

Because the car was in such great condition, he guessed some minor tinkering would have the car ready for the road. First he'd look around the barn for an oil pan and whatever else he might need, and then he'd get the rest of the stuff at an auto supply store. If he could find a For Sale sign, he'd save himself another trip.

Now that he'd inspected the classic beauty, Tanner had a hard time understanding how his father could have enjoyed laboring over their battered, ordinary truck. Tanner just knew he had been proud to help to bring the heap back to life and relished the time alone with his father.

At one time his father and grandfather must have felt that same closeness.

When ordered to abandon the woman he loved, the woman carrying his child, Tanner's father had turned his back on his parents and the family wealth. The father-and-son bond had obviously not been strong enough, thank God. Tanner didn't even want to imagine what his life might have been like if his father hadn't been so selfless and honorable.

Tanner would give anything to have his parents back in his life again, but they were gone, forever. He'd never had a choice about his loss. If Cassie was right and his grandfather had regrets about the alienation, then it was too damn bad. He could have reached out to his son at any time during the estrangement and made amends, but he'd refused to budge an inch.

Tanner had no intention of letting the old man off the hook for what he'd done to his family.

Chapter Four

Cassie stopped at the curb illuminated by a lone streetlight across the road to check for cars. Sheets of rain fell from the angry evening sky, but that only made her more determined to visit Fairfax House.

A fierce wind snatched her breath away, then changed direction and lifted her neon-orange poncho up and out. She gasped at the sudden wet pelting on her body that left her baseball cap, T-shirt, frayed shorts and sandals soaked.

Nothing she could do about it now, and she needed to check if the newly repaired roof had held up during the storm.

She gathered the drenched garment around her, took a deep breath, then darted across the empty street to the barn while sheets of rain continued to blast her.

She pounded on the massive sliding door with both fists. "Tanner, it's Cassie. Open up!"

She had hoped to postpone seeing Tanner until the

morning. Now that the chemistry between them had proven undeniable, she wanted as much time as possible to brace herself for their next encounter. But her promise to an old friend overruled her discomfort. She had worked with attractive customers before and knew how to keep things on a professional level. She had a job to do, plain and simple.

Not a problem.

Soaked from head to toe, and frustrated, she kicked at the door with the tip of her soggy sandal. "I know you're in there, Tanner."

The door suddenly slid open. A hand reached out and yanked her inside. "Are you crazy?" Tanner held on to her shoulders, his expression grim. "Don't you know it's dangerous to run around in storms?"

The word *dangerous* stuck in Cassie's mind, but had nothing to do with the weather, and everything to do with the fact she had caught Tanner shirtless. She couldn't take her eyes off his bare, broad shoulders. Fine, dark hair dusted his muscular chest. Her hands ached to reach out and explore the hard planes and taut skin, to discover if the hair was as silky as it appeared.

She folded her arms in front of her instead and struggled to find her voice. For heaven's sake, you'd think she'd never seen a man without his shirt on before. Of course she had, but Tanner was different.

A sense of power radiated from him. He'd plucked her out of the rain as if she weighed no more than the strands of straw scattered on the barn floor. His grip on her shoulders remained firm, but all she could think of was how he'd stared in bewilderment at those same hands after they had failed miserably at painting. How just hours ago, the brush of his hand against hers had left her more wobbly-kneed than her one, unforgettable experience on an uneven ladder.

Tanner's gaze, still fiercely intense, only reminded her of how those same dark eyes had reflected vulnerability when strangers had appeared on his doorstep with food and words of sympathy. To her surprise, she'd even seen those eyes sparkle with mischief while teasing her.

He was obviously a man of many layers. Just as she enjoyed stripping a piece of furniture to get to the beautiful wood, she wanted to chip away at Tanner's surface to discover what was hidden underneath. If she succeeded, would she find a treasure or something for the scrap pile?

"Cassie, answer me. What couldn't wait until tomorrow and made you risk getting out in this storm?"

Risk. A good word. A good, brisk reminder to stick to business. She backed up, and into the barn door, out of his reach. "I'm worried about your roof. Have you checked it since the rain?" She trusted her roofer, but this job was even more important than most.

"No. I got sidetracked with the car."

She peeked around his left shoulder and saw that the top had been put down. "I can understand why. It's a classic. I'll never forget the first time Mr. Frank let me drive it, to get the kinks out, or so he said. But I think—"

"Quit changing the subject. Why are you worried about the roof? I thought it was fixed."

"It is. We just haven't had any heavy rain in a while and I want to make sure. If there are still leaks, they'd have to be repaired before I can put in new wallpaper, not to mention what standing water would do to the new tile floor. It would mean delays.''

"Let's go." He grabbed his shirt from the hood of the car.

"There's no point in both of us getting soaked. If the house is open, I'll just take a quick look and you can check out the car some more.''

"I never intended to mess with the car this much. We'll both go." He pulled the shirt on over his head, his muscles rippling.

Her throat went dry. "Suit yourself." Unwilling to let their bodies touch for any reason, she heaved open the door before he could reach around her to do so himself. She held on to her hat and sprinted for the covered porch with only the dim glow of a corner streetlight to guide her way.

Tanner quickly appeared at her side. He wiped the rain off his face with his hands, then did the same to his arms. Kicking off his shoes, he opened the screen door, stepped inside and continued to hold the door open for her.

All but concern for the new floor slipped from her mind. She stepped out of her sopping wet sandals, flung off her poncho and hurried into the kitchen. Her gaze flew to the ceiling to check for leaks and she sighed with relief. Not a drop.

Good. She knelt down and ran her hands over the tiles and smiled. Dry as a cornfield in July. Even better. "Sorry for the false alarm," she said and stood.

Alarm failed to describe the look on Tanner's face. What was his problem? She was soaked to the bone and resembled a drowned rat. So what?

Irritated and a tad defensive, she folded her arms

across her chest and opened her mouth to lecture him on the impoliteness of staring. Instead, she gasped at the unexpected sticky sensation of wet cotton molded against her skin. Soaked, transparent cotton that proved an insufficient barrier to her nipples, pert and hard from the rain and the effect of the sexy man standing in front of her.

Oh, boy.

She'd been so worried about the floor, she'd forgotten about her clinging shirt. He had probably seen the *design* of the lace on her bra, for heaven's sake.

But the expected embarrassment never materialized. The pure hunger radiating from Tanner's dark eyes vanquished any urge to cover herself up and she slowly lowered her arms to her sides. The room suddenly turned warm. She struggled to find her breath and noticed Tanner battling the same problem. How had this happened? Within minutes she'd gone from feeling soggy-to-the-bone unattractive to rain-kissed desirable.

She should leave. Her feet refused to obey.

Tanner couldn't pull his gaze away from the delicate heart-shaped pattern of Cassie's lacy bra, or the dark nipples begging to be touched, kissed. He clenched his jaw as he fought against the impulse and the realization he had never wanted a woman more in his life.

A storm of emotions had raged inside him from the moment Cassie had stepped inside the barn, soaked and wearing yet another hat. She'd seemed rattled and tongue-tied, not herself at all, and he worried something was seriously wrong. A fierce protectiveness had surfaced from out of nowhere, leaving him angry over her recklessness.

Anger had quickly turned to panic, though, when she'd mentioned concerns over the roof and storm. He didn't want Cassie to have any reason to spend one day more than necessary in Fairfax House. The woman was dangerous to his peace of mind. So, he'd followed her into the house to check the roof.

His relief over the dry floor had quickly evaporated, though, at the sight of Cassie's shirt molded against her chest. She'd been just as surprised by the condition of her clothes, judging by her gasp and startled expression. But then her surprise had given way to a boldness that acknowledged she knew that he was staring and why, and didn't blame him. In fact, he'd swear she was just as hungry for him as he was for her.

He tried to convince himself it had just been too long between women, but knew the rationalization was a lie. His attraction toward Cassie ran much deeper than the physical, and was much more dangerous. She made him want things he didn't even know he wanted. She'd brought him a plant, for crying out loud. Had him picturing her at the kitchen table with a child on her lap. Their child?

Such a sobering thought hardened his resolve. "I'll get you a towel." He darted from the room before he could change his mind and give into the urge to taste her rain-kissed lips.

Minutes later he returned with a plush, white, monogrammed towel he'd found in the downstairs bathroom. He handed it to her, careful not to let their fingers touch.

"Thanks." The lightness in her voice seemed forced, as well as her smile. She wiped her face, then wrapped the towel around her shoulders. "I'll be sure and return it."

"No problem."

"I try not to work Sundays—"

"That's good. I mean, a person needs time to unwind, go out." Damn. Why had he said that?

"I agree. But I usually end up doing paperwork." She twisted the ends of the towel between her fingers. "Anyway, I guess I'll see you at nine on Monday," she said, and hurried out the door.

Now *that* was a problem. He stepped out onto the porch and watched her run into the night, taking her sandals, useless poncho and almost as worthless towel with her. Only when she had disappeared safely inside did he leave his post.

With a flick of a bolt, he locked the door against any outside intrusions, all the while aware that what he really needed protection from was Cassie. Unattached Cassie, or so he assumed. He'd given her the perfect opportunity to mention she had someone in her life, and discovered she only had paperwork to keep her company on her day off.

What was wrong with the men in this town?

No. He didn't care about her personal life.

His impractical, unacceptable attraction for the beautiful woman who wore hats and lacy bras was something he hadn't planned on. From the beginning she had him thinking unheard of mushy, romantic thoughts about campfires and walks in the rain.

At least tomorrow was Sunday and he'd be left alone. He could work on the Thunderbird, maybe take it for a drive.

Keeping busy didn't solve his real problem,

though. How was he going to be able to keep resisting Cassie, day in and day out?

Cassie sprayed hot water onto a small section of faded wallpaper and let it soak for a few minutes. Unfortunately, the spray of water reminded her of her late-night dash in the rain on Saturday to Fairfax House, and the waiting gave her time to relive the wet T-shirt fiasco.

"Yoo-hoo," a familiar high-pitched voice called out from the front of Fairfax House. The doorbell rang twice. Cassie smiled and put down her scraper. Tanner wouldn't know what hit him after a few rounds with Mrs. Boone.

The sound of Tanner's boots pounding against the stairs soon followed. Cassie hurried to the door that separated the kitchen from the front of the house and shamelessly eavesdropped.

"Mrs. Boone. What is all that stuff? Let me help."

"No, no. It'll all spill. Just hold the door open for me."

Cassie grinned, pleased to have Mrs. Boone as an ally. On Sunday, Cassie had made a point of spending some time with her landlady who thrived on her role as town historian. As innocently as possible, Cassie had steered the conversation toward the older woman's passion.

Before long, Mrs. Boone had come up with the idea to drop by Fairfax House the following afternoon with material Tanner might find interesting.

Cassie had then called her mother who revealed she'd already made plans to invite Tanner to dinner. Next, Cassie had set up an appointment with her loan officer at the bank. If she failed to convince Tanner to stay, she intended to buy the house herself. She'd turn it into a boardinghouse until she had a family of her own. Although she doubted such drastic measures would prove necessary, she wanted to cover all bases.

"What's this all about, Mrs. Boone?"

Cassie heard the frustration in Tanner's voice, but his chilly greeting that morning made it easy to ignore the temptation to take pity on him. He had let her inside the house at nine, his gaze never meeting hers. Then, with barely a nod in her direction, he had disappeared up the stairs. Whereas she had hoped to make light of the heated situation they had found themselves in on Saturday, Tanner had opted for the cold shoulder.

She told herself the jab of pain located somewhere near her heart didn't mean that she'd been hurt by his icy reception, or that she had taken the snub as a rejection of her and what had passed between them two nights before.

No, she was just concerned because he was distancing himself and she worried she'd blown her chance to fulfill her promise to Mr. Frank. She was simply frustrated. After all, it wasn't as if she had actually hoped that the experience was as heady and unique for him as it had been for her.

Yeah, right.

As the voices and footsteps grew nearer, Cassie scurried back to her workplace and picked up her scraper. She had recruited the town's historian for Tanner's own good. Shoot, he might even thank her later for making it easier for him to learn more about his family's history.

"Cassie, dear. Nice to see you," Mrs. Boone

greeted as she entered the kitchen and dropped her armload of leather-bound scrapbooks and photo albums on the table. As always, her orange hair rested in a neat pile on top of her head; heavy makeup matted her lined face. The kind but pushy woman surveyed the kitchen like a queen bee might inspect her hive. "Looks like it's coming along nicely, Cassie. I see you almost have that horrid wallpaper down. I never did like it. Too stuffy."

Amen. "I should finish stripping the wallpaper today. Tomorrow I'll finish priming the rest of the woodwork."

"Have you picked out the new wallpaper yet?"

"I'm bringing some samples tomorrow, but Tanner left the choice up to me."

"A smart man, I see. Just like his daddy."

Cassie glanced at Tanner, standing tall with his hands on lean hips, his attention glued to the books on the table. She couldn't help but wonder if his daddy had filled out a T-shirt so well, or made a pair of jeans look so sexy.

Memories of Saturday night came back with a vengeance. Until Tanner, no man had ever made her ache with the desire to touch him. No man had ever looked at her as if he wanted to devour her. Her own boldness in reaction to the raw hunger in his eyes had left her not only surprised and a little frightened, but exhilarated as well. What would have happened if he hadn't done the sensible thing and walked away?

She wasn't sure, and that bothered her.

Mrs. Boone turned to Tanner. "I saw the sign in the yard. It's a pity you have to sell. Just won't be the same. At least with new wallpaper, you'll attract more buyers.''

Cassie had chosen to say nothing about the sign to Tanner, but she couldn't deny how the sight of it had made her stomach feel as heavy as a bag of fast-setting concrete.

"I hope so. Mrs. Boone, we're both kind of busy, so—"

"Of course, young man. Now, as I always say, there's no better time than the present to get to know the past. I just knew you'd want to see these. I am the town historian, you know. New Haven's entire history is chronicled in these books, and your family is very prominent."

"How...nice of you, Mrs. Boone. But you should keep the books, since I don't know when I'll get to them."

Mrs. Boone had finagled more free repairs from Cassie than she cared to admit. She counted on Mrs. Boone's track record of pestering or guilting a person into doing what she wanted.

"Nonsense. Look at this one first, though, because it features your daddy." Mrs. Boone picked a worn, black scrapbook from the middle of the pile and flipped it open. Cassie walked over to the table, full of curiosity over Tanner's reaction. She'd seen the albums a hundred times and enjoyed the old stories. A peek into his parents' past would surely prove ir-resistible to Tanner.

The opened page held several newspaper articles detailing his father's still unbroken record for most yards passed in a game, along with a photo of him in his football uniform.

Mrs. Boone sighed. "Such a handsome young

man. Sweet as could be, and you obviously follow in his footsteps. I meant to tell you before this, but thank you for being so kind to Mrs. Johnson the other day. She gets confused, and seeing you made her think of your daddy. He was one of her favorites.''

He shrugged. "No big deal.''

Cassie and the rest of the town knew of Mrs. Johnson's wandering mind and looked out for her. But a stranger? Tanner? Cassie didn't know what to make of his softer side. He must save his moodiness for her.

"Oh, but it is. Lots of people don't have the patience for old, confused people. Want to lock them up somewhere. Why the other day—''

"Thanks a lot, Mrs. Boone,'' Tanner interrupted. A tight smile on his face, he took her by the elbow and led her out of the kitchen. "I'll make sure the books get returned.''

"No hurry. Tootles, Cassie.''

"Goodbye, Mrs. Boone.''

While Tanner walked Mrs. Boone to the door, Cassie thumbed through the scrapbook to find a picture of the original Fairfax House. Many renovations had been done through the years, but just as the family had weathered good times and bad, the noble lines of the house had endured.

Footsteps on the stairs caught her attention. She hurried out to the hallway. "Tanner, where are you going?''

He paused and turned toward her. "Why? Is there a problem?''

Her only problem stood on the stairs. She glared at him. "You're not even going to look at the books? There's a picture of this house when it was first built by *your* ancestors. Doesn't family mean anything to you?''

He frowned. ''My family, my parents, meant everything to me. But they're gone. Fairfax House is just a house made of wood, stone and glass, like any other.''

She swallowed her panic while her mind raced to think of a way to make him understand all that Fairfax House could give him: not just safety from the elements, but ties to his family, an instant connection to the town. Roots. ''You're wrong, Tanner, and I'm going to prove it to you.''

''Forget it, Cassie. I'm going—''

''No, wait.'' She crossed over into the dining room to the hutch where she knew emergency supplies were kept. The flashlight refused to work. Darn. Dead batteries, no doubt. She needed a light. Quick. Before Tanner disappeared.

She settled for the next best thing, a candle and book of matches, and rushed back to the stairs.

''A candle? You're wasting my time.''

''Just give me five minutes.''

''If I do, then will you leave me alone?''

''Sure. Come on. I want to show you something.'' She headed for the closet under the stairway, looking over her shoulder to ensure he had followed. Impatient and scowling, he quickly shortened the distance between them.

Cassie opened the door, used her foot as a wedge to keep it from closing and lit the candle.

''What's this about, Cassie? You might start a fire with that darned thing.''

''Relax. I just want to show you something. The

closet light shorted out a long time ago and was never fixed. Just follow me and watch your head.''

She entered the closet, protecting the flame with a cupped hand. Just a hint of the scent of mothballs laced the lifeless air. Candlelight flickered across the top shelf cluttered with hatboxes gray from dust, and a free-for-all pile of scarves and gloves. A rod bowed under the weight of coats ranging from windbreakers to down-filled parkas.

She turned to the right, ducked and took a few more steps into the narrowing closet. She sat on a trunk and waved for Tanner to follow. "Look," she said, and held the candle up toward the wall.

"I can't see. What is it?"

"Come closer."

He bent at the waist and knees and groaned. "What's so important that I need to risk a concussion for?" He tested the strength of the small chest and then sat, his shoulder brushing against hers. His nearness created a heat inside her that could light a thousand candles, and left her more off balance than the dark ever could.

The excitement building inside her had nothing to do with the fact she was alone, in close quarters and semidarkness, with the sexiest man she'd ever met. No, she was just eager to show him proof that the house was special.

She took his hand and placed it on top of the familiar etchings. "You won't find this in any other house, Tanner. These were put here by your father when he was sixteen and in love for the first time."

"'FF loves DA. Forever,'" Tanner read in a whisper as he traced the carving with the tips of his fingers.

Thoughts of the past disappeared from Cassie's mind and all she could think about was how much she wanted to feel those same fingertips brushing against her skin. How much she wanted to hear him murmur *her* name in the darkness.

"Who's DA?"

The sound of Tanner's voice jolted Cassie back to reality, reminded her of why she had coaxed him into the closet in the first place. "Diane Arnold. My mother. Your dad and my mom were high school sweethearts. This very spot is where they shared their first kiss. Isn't that incredible?"

Tanner pulled his gaze away from the crude carving and stared at Cassie outlined in candlelight. *She* was incredible. He had yet to witness her doing anything in half measures. She didn't just employ workers, she knew and cared about them. A pastry wasn't just breakfast, but a savored treat. She seemed intent on proving to him the value of a particular house, and had braved a storm to check on a job site. The image of her, soaked to the skin and boldly returning his hungry stare had haunted him the past two nights.

Instead of a day of rest, he'd spent Sunday jogging through town and then paced the huge, empty house in a futile effort to clear his mind of Cassie.

She was warmth and light and the most sensual woman he'd ever met. He for damned sure shouldn't be sitting next to her in such close, dark quarters where he could lose himself in her crisp citrusy fragrance that made him think of sunny skies, fresh air and a secluded picnic for two. Her face glowed in the candlelight; her eyes shined with amusement. Her mouth was curved in a dreamy smile.

Who cared about the past? He could only think

about how much he wanted to kiss *her*. Now. The
sound of Cassie's ragged breathing that matched his
own drowned out the warning bells; the semidarkness hid the red flags.

Chapter Five

Tanner cupped Cassie's face in his hands and gave in to the need to taste her lips. A sigh escaped her sweet mouth, welcoming him into her world. A slow exploration quickly gave way to an urgent search of each sensitive corner.

He had known chemistry existed between them, but this went beyond the typical spark to a powerful connection. He couldn't get enough; he wanted to know everything about her. Every thought, every secret.

He was on fire, like he'd never been before. Funny, though, how his one knee felt a good ten degrees hotter than the rest of him. Not exactly the part of his anatomy he'd expected to suffer.

He reluctantly tore his mouth away from Cassie's and glanced down to find the blasted candle resting against his knee. "Damn," he muttered and grabbed the candle from her hand. How could he have let this happen?

Cassie's eyes fluttered open. She looked dazed. "What, what's wrong?"

"It's nothing. Just some melted wax."

Her gaze darted from the candle to his leg. Her eyes widened. "I'm so sorry. I—I—you—the kiss. I guess I lost my head for a minute."

She wasn't the only one, Tanner cursed silently. "Maybe we'd better get out of here before things go too far."

He escaped to the front porch for some much needed air and space; he gripped the railing to hide his unsteady hands. More than breathing room, though, he needed to find a way to keep from falling under Cassie's spell. With or without a flammable object in her hand, she was one dangerous woman.

A siren wailed in the distance, but he couldn't tell if it belonged to an ambulance or a fire truck. Luckily, the candle had dripped or the 911 call might have come from Fairfax House.

Twenty-seven more days. Surely he could survive that amount of time without any more close calls.

Mrs. Boone appeared on her porch, a phone attached to one ear as she hurried toward him. Now what?

"Tanner, is Cassie still here?"

"Yes. Why?"

"Don't you worry, Mardell. Your husband is a tough old bird. See you in a bit," Mrs. Boone said into the phone, then tucked it inside an apron pocket.

The front door punched open and Cassie dashed outside. The mouth that had moments before been curved in a dreamy smile, now formed a grim line. Had the kiss upset her that much? He expected some sort of reaction—after all, he'd been shaken, too—

but she seemed almost defensive. He wished his busybody neighbor would leave so he could reassure Cassie that the mistake wouldn't be repeated.

"Tanner, I've got to go." Her gaze flew from him to Mrs. Boone. "Oh, hello, Mrs. Boone. Did you hear about Pete?"

She nodded. "I saw your van and figured you were here and would want to know."

Confused, Tanner looked from one woman to the other, annoyed that a part of him hoped Cassie's grim mood had more to do with whatever news she'd heard rather than their kiss. "Know what?"

"Mr. Campbell had an accident," Cassie said. "He was working out at the festival site and somehow lost his balance. They think his ankle is sprained if not broken."

Mrs. Boone put her hand on Tanner's arm. "Mr. Campbell owns Camp's Drive-In at the end of town," she explained in a hushed voice. "He always lets the town use the land behind his place for the festival. We bring in rides, food and bingo tents, things like that. And he always puts up the stage for the Homecoming Court and the bands. Real handy like that, or at least, he was. The poor man."

A memory flickered in Tanner's mind. "Are you talking about the ice-cream place, just before the turnoff to the highway?"

"You know of it?" Mrs. Boone asked, smiling. "Of course, they do sell ice cream, but they also have the best wingding basket ever. Why, I know..."

Tanner tuned out the older lady's rambling. He was suddenly five years old again, on his first visit to Fairfax House. He remembered how tightly his father had held his hand as they maneuvered steps which had seemed the size of mountains.

Vaguely, he recalled reciting the alphabet to the old man introduced as Grandfather, and how the conversation between him and his father had escalated to a shouting match.

Tanner had never seen his father so angry, not even when he had spilled juice on their new rug. His father had scooped him up into his arms and whisked him out of the dark house and into their pickup.

He had cried, afraid he'd done something wrong. His father stopped the truck long enough to comfort him and insist he was the best kid that ever walked the earth. Some things just weren't meant to be, he explained, and offered to buy him an ice-cream cone before the long drive back to Texas. No more tears.

Soon he was sitting on his father's lap at a bright-red table under a red-and-white umbrella. The chocolate coating on his soft vanilla ice cream had spread like lava down the sides of his mountain-size cone. He could feel his father's chest quake as he chuckled over his son's futile attempt to stay one lick ahead of the melting mess.

"Don't worry, young man. It'll all come off in the wash," a stranger had said as he drew near. "I thought it was you, Frankie, but wasn't quite sure. Been a long time, friend. How've you been? How's Susan?"

The men shook hands and clapped one another on the back. "We're both great, Pete. And this is my son, Tanner."

Pete had crouched down until eye level with Tanner. "Looks like you've had a rough day, partner. Nothing like ice cream to make things right again."

Tanner had nodded while he continued to lick his cone.

"It's always a rough day when it comes to my old man," his dad had replied. "Some things never change. And now Tanner is in the middle. Poor guy thinks the blowout was his fault." His dad had hugged him so tightly he almost lost the ice-cream cone. "It wasn't your fault, sport," he'd said, "you did just fine."

"But I didn't get to finish my ABCs, cause you and Grandfather were yelling, and I heard my name."

"Your grandfather loves you, Tanner, it's just that…" His dad turned to Pete as if hoping he'd have the answer.

Pete's smile had turned sad. "It's sort of like when you caught your first frog or butterfly, Tanner. Have you ever done that?"

Tanner had nodded. "Sure. But you have to be quick. I caught a real cool butterfly last year."

Pete had nodded. "Did you let it go right away?"

Tanner had shaken his head. "Not the first time. It was so pretty I wanted to keep it, but I must've held it too tight, 'cause it died. I didn't mean to kill it, honest. Just wanted to keep it with me. So the next time I caught one, I let it go."

"Well, some people can't let go, even if it means losing what they want most in the world. And some people don't learn their lesson, like you did. See, you're smart, like your daddy. And maybe, just maybe, some day your grandpa will get smart, too. Do you understand?"

"I think so," Tanner had replied, even though he

wondered how anyone could compare his old, wrinkled grandfather to a beautiful butterfly.

Tanner remembered how funny his dad's voice had sounded when he'd thanked Pete.

"Tanner?"

Gentle shaking on his arm pulled him back to the present and an impatient Cassie. "Tanner, did you hear me? I'm sorry if you don't understand, but I've got to go now. I'll come a few hours earlier in the morning or stay later to make up the time."

"Understand what? Go where?"

"Pete Campbell is the sweetest man on earth. He's probably in the hospital by now, but I can't do anything for him there, anyway. What I can do is go work at the site while it's still light out. He'll worry himself sick if he thinks everything won't be ready in time for the festival." Cassie turned to the neighbor. "You'll get word to him that we're taking care of things, won't you, Mrs. Boone?"

"Of course, dear. I was going to go sit with Mardell, anyway, so I'll tell her and she'll let him know."

"Thanks. And give Pete our best."

"I will. Bye, now."

Tanner couldn't even remember what Pete looked like, but he'd never forget the kindness he'd shown a scared little boy. "I'm coming with you, Cassie."

Cassie froze, certain she had heard Tanner wrong. "Why?" She wanted as much space as possible between them. Of course she hated that Pete had gotten hurt, but she'd been grateful for a legitimate excuse to leave Fairfax House, for a distraction to keep her mind off Tanner's earth-shattering kiss.

Even now, she fought the urge to put her fingers

to her lips. His strong hands had gently framed her face before he had deliberately claimed her mouth with a breath-stealing kiss. She could still taste him. Somehow, she hadn't been surprised to discover nothing sloppy or tentative about a first kiss from Tanner. His tender, confident exploration had made her feel safe, desirable, cherished. All resistance had melted away. Fortunately, so had the candle.

"Forget it, Cassie. I'll take my truck."

His curt response assured her the kiss had been forgotten. Good. The kiss should never have happened and she needed to quit obsessing, put the focus back on why she had led him to the closet in the first place.

If she took her personal feelings out of the equation, she could see that Pete's misfortune offered her an opportunity to help Tanner feel more connected to the town and its people. "Wait. Of course you can ride with me. You just took me by surprise, that's all. I was all set to defend why I had to leave early. It never occurred to me that you'd want to come. Let's face it, from the minute you arrived in town, you haven't acted interested in anything or anyone around here."

"It's no act."

She forced herself not to react. Where was the tender, passionate man who had kissed her senseless? Too bad she was all out of dripping candles. "Then why bother?"

Tanner shifted his weight from one foot to another. "Let's just say I believe in returning favors."

Cassie yearned to ask more questions, but the firm line of his mouth convinced her to wait for a better time. Maybe Pete could shed some light on the mystery, after he was on the mend. Knowing Pete, he wouldn't be out of commission for long.

"Let's go, then." Cassie led the way to her van parked along the curb at the side of the house. Giving Tanner a ride to Pete's was no problem. The ride was short; getting Tanner involved would help Pete and further her cause to make Tanner feel connected to New Haven.

She hopped in, tossed some sample books in the back and stuffed some fast-food wrappers under the seat. Tanner settled in the passenger seat and belted up. "It's like an art gallery in here." Tanner inspected the collage of pictures attached to both visors and a coffee mug plastered with a girl's smiling face.

"I spend a lot of time in this van. It's nice being surrounded by friendly faces." She pointed to the mug in the drink holder. "This one never fails to make me smile. Could you look at that precious face and do anything but?"

"Probably not. Who is it?"

She could swear she saw the corners of Tanner's mouth inch upward, just a little. "Georgie's daughter, Emily. Cute as a button, smart, and wraps everyone she meets around her little finger. She reminds me of my sister. Jill has always had this effortless ability to make people like her." Although her divorce had changed her quite a bit. Cassie hoped it was just a matter of time before her sister reverted back to her usual outgoing self.

"And you don't?"

Cassie shrugged, started the van and pulled out of the driveway. "I'm more selective and don't think some people are worth my time. I'm not crushed if someone doesn't take a liking to me, whereas Jill would see that as a challenge, whether she liked that person or not." Cassie checked for traffic at the four-way stop, then turned right down Main Street which ran the length of the town.

A few minutes later she turned into the gravel driveway of Camp's Drive-In. Tanner sat up straighter and gazed intently out his window.

"Have you been here before, Tanner?"

"Once."

She'd never known anyone so guarded. What was he afraid of? Her curiosity continued to take a beating. "Then you can see, nothing much has changed. Old tables and umbrellas are always replaced with more of the same. Just don't ever mention changing colors to Pete. Someone suggested livening up the place with blue and yellow, instead of the red and white, and I thought poor Pete was going to faint." She smiled at the memory. "He lives in the house next door and said he's the one who looks at the things more than anyone, so he decides."

She veered left of the drive-in, followed a dirt road out to a field, and stopped next to a huge oak tree that was rumored to be older than the town. Stacks of lumber and cinder blocks were off to the left, and to the right stood a makeshift workbench made out of two sawhorses and a sheet of plywood.

With a wave she hopped out of the van and approached an elderly man wearing a Howard's Lumber cap. "Hello, Mr. Howard."

"Hey, Cassie, girl! What are you doing here?"

Several older teenage boys sat on the ground chewing on blades of grass. Ben Denton wore his usual frown. Shy Allen Smith stared at his shoes.

And Cory Jennings, never still, was all energy and grins.

"I heard about Pete and came to help out."

The old man squinted at Tanner. "And you must be that Fairfax boy. Some funny first name. I for darned sure can't think of it at the moment."

Tanner shook the man's outstretched hand. "The name is Tanner, sir."

"Oh, yes. That's it. Saw the For Sale sign. Cryin' shame. So, you know Pete, do ya?"

"We've met."

"What can we do to help, Mr. Howard?"

The older man threw up his hands. "Cassie, I'm not sure. I don't know nothing about building, I just sell the stuff. I think Pete's supposed to be teaching these boys about tools and such. They were just getting started on the stage when Pete took a fall. Is young Fairfax here going to take over?"

Tanner's gaze drifted to the boys, hovered for a long moment, then turned to Cassie. "Any blueprints?"

Cassie shook her head. "But I can tell you what we need." She could build the thing in her sleep, but wanted Tanner to take charge. "We build the stage in pieces so we can reuse it, but this is the year for a new one. Pete stores most of the materials in his barn behind his house next door." She gave Tanner a rough idea of the layout for the festival, but didn't offer any suggestions.

"Okay, guys, listen up." The crew of three jumped up and hurried over to Tanner. "First, we need to know names. I'm Tanner." The boys introduced themselves.

"Exactly what kind of program is this supposed to be?" Tanner asked.

"We get credit toward shop class this fall and service hours for helping to build the festival stage," Cory explained. "We're supposed to learn how to measure and how to use tools."

Ben smirked. "Only now we probably won't be able to. We're just wasting our time. Might as well go home."

Cassie heard the challenge behind Ben's comment. She didn't know the boy, but everyone knew his dad, John Denton, a former basketball and baseball star of New Haven and now a hotshot attorney. If she wasn't mistaken, his wife had left him years ago for some drummer in a band.

Her heart went out to Ben. No mom, and a dad that cast a long shadow. Would Tanner know how to deal with a troubled teenager?

Tanner met Ben's gaze. "Not so fast, Ben. I started out in the construction business when I was about your age. I went on to become a master carpenter and I own a construction company now, so I think I can handle teaching you guys the basics. But it's up to you."

"That would be great, sir," Cory said, and nudged Ben.

"Yeah. Great."

Allen nodded his consent.

Cassie breathed a sigh of relief. Tanner had obviously thought his offer of help for Pete would involve construction of some sort, not instruction for a trio of teenage boys, one with a major attitude problem. Thank goodness Tanner had accepted the challenge.

"Let's get something straight, then," Tanner continued. "I'm only filling in until Mr. Campbell is able to come back, and since I'm the new person here, if anyone has any comments or suggestions, speak up. The first thing we'll do is go over the various tools we're going to use. I'll briefly tell you what each one does, but I won't get real specific until we're actually using the tools." Tanner walked over to the workbench and the boys followed.

"Cassie, could you find some paper and pencil and sketch out the details of the stage for me?"

"Sure." Cassie left for her van, smiling so hard her face hurt.

Pete could focus on getting well, now that Tanner had agreed to take on the project and the role of mentor to the boys. Soon, a sense of belonging would pull him under and he'd surrender to the inevitable—New Haven was his home.

Tanner had stepped into quicksand, and didn't even know it.

Cassie finished her assigned task and took the rough blueprint to Tanner. She found him brainstorming with the boys on how to make a sawhorse, a basic and useful project.

She admired Tanner's respectful handling of the boys, although his confident manner didn't surprise her at all. Anyone that kissed the way he did—no, she wouldn't think about that.

Tanner noticeably relaxed the longer he remained outside. He made an effort to get to know the boys, asking them questions about school and sports. Cory and Allen puffed up with pride from all the attention. Ben, though, remained sullen.

While Tanner worked with the boys, Cassie transferred the cinder blocks to the roped-out stage area in approximate positions. The blocks would support the stage floor.

"Okay guys, time for a break," Tanner announced several hours later.

"Actually, sir, we've got to go," informed the tallest boy, Cory. "We have a baseball game in an hour. We already cleared it with Mr. Campbell, though, I swear."

"No problem. You did great work today." Tanner shook hands with each of them. "What was your arrangement with Mr. Campbell for the rest of the time?"

"We hired on for nine to five until he doesn't need us anymore," Cory said.

"Great. Then we'll see you tomorrow. Nine o'clock."

Cassie helped Tanner clean up the work site, then drove him back to Fairfax House. "So, I couldn't help but overhear that you're planning to be at the site tomorrow."

"Is there a problem?"

"Not at all. But they'll be counting on you to see this through. Are you sure you want to make such a commitment?"

"Just until Mr. Campbell gets back on his feet."

"That's fair. I'll pitch in when I can and you'll get help from the rest of the town." She stopped her truck in front of his house. "By the way, you were great with the boys. You really had their attention and seemed to know when to stop talking and let them work."

Tanner shrugged. "They're young and have lots of energy."

Humble. She liked that in a person.

"I'll bring my own tools tomorrow, and it'll go even better," he added. "I should probably get my hands on another cordless screwdriver so they can each have one."

"I'll ask Mr. Howard to donate them and bring them by. He likes to keep busy and usually visits the site every day."

"Thanks. And thanks for the ride."

"No problem. But I do need to come in and get my bag. We left in such a hurry this afternoon that I forgot, and that's where I keep my book with all my appointments in it. Without my planner, I'm lost." She followed him up the sidewalk to the front door. "Just so you know, tomorrow I'll finish priming the woodwork. Once it dries, the next thing is two coats of paint. You might want to leave your windows open because of the fumes."

Tanner stopped abruptly. She rocked back on her heels to keep from running into him. "What's wrong?"

"The door isn't shut all the way. I rushed out of here so fast, I'm not sure if I locked it or not. Someone must've broken in while we were gone."

"Don't be so suspicious, Tanner. This is a main street with its share of traffic. We tore out of here so fast, who knows if the door shut or not?"

"Stay behind me, just in case." Tanner entered the house and gave each room a cursory glance as he made his way down the hall. He rushed inside the den and turned in a circle as he checked every corner of the room. "Someone's been here. My stuff is gone. Why would they steal my sleeping bag and leave the antiques? And what is that great smell?"

Cassie smiled. "My guess is fried chicken. I've got a pretty good idea who our visitor was. Hang on."

"Wait. It could be dangerous."

Cassie chuckled. "I know. But not in the way you mean." She hurried into the kitchen and Tanner followed. On the table, tucked under a plate piled with fried chicken, peeked a note written in all too familiar handwriting on the back of a long grocery receipt. "'Heard you were out helping Pete,'" Cassie read aloud. "'Thought you'd be hungry. Salad is in fridge, the front door was open, hope you don't mind. Moved you into your dad's old room—more comfy! Dinner Thursday, my place. Ask Cassie for details. My girl does great work, doesn't she? So sad that you're selling, though. Can't wait to meet you. Hugs, D.'"

"What's going on? Who is this D person? And why would she just waltz on in?"

Cassie grinned with pride. In one swoop, her mother had offered nourishment for the moment and the future, provided comfort and plugged her daughter's business. "You haven't been robbed, you've been taken under the wing of my mom, the ultimate mother hen. She wouldn't think twice about coming inside. Remember, she used to work here and was treated like family."

"That doesn't give her the right to move my stuff. I was just fine camping out in the den."

"You'd never convince her. And you're here for a month—"

"Twenty-seven days."

"Whatever. That's a long time to 'camp out.' If you don't like the room she put you in, move back!"

"That's not the point. She shouldn't have interfered."

Cassie shrugged. "Fine. You can tell her yourself at dinner on Thursday."

"No, *you* can tell her thanks, but no thanks."

Cassie swallowed her disappointment over finding that the walls around Tanner, which had crumbled under the pressure of fresh air, hard labor and camaraderie, had reappeared with a vengeance. "Aren't you the least bit curious to meet one of your dad's high school sweethearts? She'll have so many stories to tell about your parents, your head will spin. And if you don't show up for dinner, not only will *I* never hear the end of it, but you won't, either. She'll pester you until you agree."

Curiosity flickered in his eyes before indifference returned. "She won't just drop it?"

"No way."

He hesitated. "If that's the only way I'll be left alone—"

"Good decision," Cassie interrupted, before he could change his mind. "Dinner is at seven, but I have to warn you about our family tradition. Thursday nights we bake bread to give to the homeless shelter. My sister usually helps, but she hasn't been around lately, so Mom will try to rope you into volunteering."

"You're kidding. I don't know anything about baking bread."

"No problem. She's used to that, since I'm all thumbs in the kitchen. You're welcome to ride with me, or I'll give you directions."

"Directions," he answered quickly.

Cassie held back a smile, amused by his attempt to seize at least some control over the evening. Wasted effort. Before the night ended, her mom would have him elbow-deep in flour.

Chapter Six

Tanner double-checked the address. Perfectly tended flower beds provided splashes of color against the small house painted a soft yellow. A swing on the porch invited him to take a load off.

Very cozy. Must be the right place.

He grabbed the bottle of wine, left the pickup and headed for the front door. What if Cassie's mom didn't drink? He certainly had no desire to offend her. He'd been taught to never show up empty-handed when invited somewhere; he knew wine was an appropriate hostess gift, so why was he second-guessing himself?

Cassie's smiling face suddenly appeared in his mind. He recalled the amusement in her voice as she read the note from her mom. The two were obviously close.

He raised his hand to knock. The door opened to reveal the real Cassie who was even more beautiful than the one pictured in his mind. No hat this time, but a wide, bright-yellow scarf that held back her riot of long, beautiful curls.

Dressed in a white blouse with yellow flower buttons, white jeans and sandals, she looked comfortable and, well, great. He was glad he had swapped his usual T-shirt for a shirt with a collar, even though Cassie had assured him dinner was casual.

She smiled, but her gaze was tinged with sadness and he swallowed the urge to ask her what was wrong so he could try to make it better. He must have sunstroke or something. Her mood wasn't his problem.

Without thinking, he reached out to touch a soft curl. "Do you ever let it go?"

She blinked. "Wh-what do you mean?"

"Your hair. It's beautiful. But it's always hidden under some hat or pulled back."

"I—I started out wearing hats because my dad always had one on. Mom gave up the fight and bought me girl hats. Besides, I'm always doing something where I need to keep my hair out of the way. I should probably cut it, but I don't have the nerve."

"I'm glad." Oh, man. Why had he said that? It was none of his business. He let go of the silky lock and quickly put his hand in a pocket. "I mean, you should do whatever you want."

"Thanks, I think I will. I'm glad you could make it, tonight, Tanner. This means a lot to my mom."

Tanner was relieved to see at least a little of the sparkle in her eyes had returned. "You made it sound like I didn't have much choice," he teased.

"You got that right." Cassie leaned toward him. "I need to warn you, though," she whispered.

"Mom is in a strange mood. She gets melancholy when she thinks too much about the past."

"Cassie, where are your manners?" a soft, feminine voice called out from somewhere to his left. "Invite our guest in."

"Coming, Mom." Cassie gestured for Tanner to step inside then closed the door. Tanner could've sworn he had entered an Italian restaurant. The unmistakable smell of garlic, onion, tomatoes and bread filled the air. His stomach growled. "Something smells great."

"Dinner will be ready soon, but Mom thought you might like to visit a little first. She's set up in the living room." Cassie walked down a short hallway then turned left.

Set up? What did that mean? Tanner wondered as he followed Cassie. He'd expected a formal room, but was pleasantly surprised. Although the furniture had elegant lines, the fabric was slightly worn and faded, nothing like the pieces at Fairfax House that screamed, "Look, but don't touch."

A camelback sofa sat at an angle in front of an oak wall unit, its doors open and shelves a jumbled mess of photo albums and scrapbooks. Piles of boxes and books covered the coffee table and end tables, but where was Cassie's mom?

"I've looked everywhere and can't find it." A petite blonde appeared from behind the sofa. He'd expected an older version of Cassie, but they shared few physical traits, if any.

The smile on her face slipped for a fraction of a second. Her right hand flew to the base of her throat. Tears formed in dark-blue eyes and she made no attempt to hide them. "Frankie's son," she murmured, then quickly enfolded him in a bear hug. She smelled of roses fresh out of the garden. "Welcome home."

Home? This wasn't home, but he couldn't deny how good the words sounded, how great a mother's hug felt, even if she wasn't his own.

She finally released him and took a step back, wiping the tears from her cheeks with the back of a hand. "Cassie tried to warn me. I'm a mess..." Her voice trailed off.

He thought she was beautiful, with her kind eyes and warm smile. No wonder his father had fallen for her at one time.

She took a deep breath. "I'm sorry. Where are my manners? I'm Diane Leighton. Thank you so much for coming."

"I'm Tanner, and I'm the one who should be thanking you. The chicken and potato salad you left were great. I brought you this." He held out the bottle of wine.

She smiled, but with obvious effort. "How wonderful. I'll chill this and we'll have it for dinner. I hope you like lasagna." She turned to her daughter. "Cassie, hon, show him one of the scrapbooks. I'll be right back."

Cassie motioned for him to sit on the couch and handed him a faded red leather scrapbook.

"Is your mom okay?"

"Sure, just a little emotional. Sort of runs in the family. My poor dad was outnumbered by us girls and never knew when the tears would start. One of us was usually upset about something."

Tanner had never met anyone as free with emotion as Cassie and her mom. His dad was a typical guy who rarely showed his feelings and his mother had survived her painful childhood with a quiet strength that refused to allow emotions to rule her life. She always said she'd never really started living until she met his father.

Cassie opened the scrapbook to the first page. "Mom thought you'd enjoy seeing pictures of your dad when he was little. Your grandparents were movers and shakers in this town, so your dad was photographed along with them."

"You shouldn't have gone to all this trouble."

"No problem. We look at the books all the time. That's why I recognized you right off."

"Oh, good, you started with one of my favorites," Diane said as she swept back into the room. Although her eyes still held a hint of sadness, she had obviously redone her makeup and had used the time to compose herself.

She sat next to Tanner and told a story about each photo or newspaper article. "I was so sorry to hear about your dad and Susan." Diane put her hand on Tanner's arm. "And with your grandfather too ill to send for you, it must have been a horrible time for you."

He stiffened at the mention of his grandfather. Upon the death of his parents, officials had informed him that his grandfather had been contacted but was unable to take him in. Tanner had let the rejection roll off him. He wouldn't have gone to live with his grandfather even if asked. Later on, when letters did arrive from his grandfather, they remained unopened and were wadded up into a paper ball and thrown into the trash can for an easy two points.

Now, he was being told his grandfather had been

too ill to take care of anyone else. If Tanner had read the letters, he might have discovered that years ago.

So his grandfather was innocent for once. Big deal. "I survived."

Diane nodded. "The strong ones do, somehow. It's never easy though. When I lost Cassie's father... No, I'd rather talk of happier things. Look at this picture of your dad in his football uniform. So handsome. And look at this one...."

Cassie had settled on the floor next to the couch and seemed content to mostly listen, her one arm resting on her mother's leg. He marveled how at ease the two were with one another. The cozy scene brought back vivid memories of his own family and how close they had been. The past fifteen years on his own had dimmed his memory, though, which was probably for the best. "I haven't seen any pictures of my mom," Tanner said, after looking through several more yearbooks. "Didn't she go to the same school?"

Regret filled Diane's gaze. "Yes, but her family was very poor. Susan would usually disappear on picture day, and I suspect now it was because she was embarrassed by her clothes. Of course then I was a self-absorbed teenager and never gave it a thought. I was never unkind to your mom, you understand, but I didn't go out of my way to be nice or help her, either. But she was obviously a special lady if your dad chose her."

"She was great."

The woman next to him was a special lady, also, or her initials wouldn't be interwoven with his father's in a dark closet under a staircase. Tanner stole a quick look at Cassie, recalling their own explosive kiss under the same cloak of darkness and if the flush of her skin was a sign, she was remembering the same thing.

"What's the first memory you have, Tanner?" Diane asked. "Where did you grow up? Did your dad tell you corny jokes like he used to in school?"

Tanner filled her in on the first seventeen years of his life, choosing only the lighter, happier memories to share. He avoided any mention of his grandfather and his obsession to have his grandson live with him; how the stream of bribes and threats had brought his mom to tears and made his dad feel guilty—he should never have tried to reconcile with his old man.

A horrible buzzing sound erupted from the kitchen. Diane jumped up from the couch. "Dinnertime! You can wash up in the bathroom down the hall to the right. Just follow your nose to the kitchen when you're done."

Tanner watched her scurry from the room, a part of him wishing she'd come back. She brought with her a warmth, a comfortableness that he hadn't experienced since he'd lost his mom. So many years had passed, he could hardly recall her face.

"Tanner, are you okay?"

"I wish I had a picture of her."

"You mean your mom?"

Tanner blinked, unaware he'd spoken out loud. "It's no big deal. After they died, stuff sort of disappeared. I just thought that while I was in town I'd try to find one." He stood and rubbed his hands together; if he didn't move or do something, he risked getting all weepy himself. "Sure smells good. Which way to wash up?"

* * *

Thirty minutes later, Tanner wiped his mouth with his napkin and laid it on the table. "Mrs. Leighton, that was the best meal I've had in a long time. Thank you."

"Call me Diane, please, and you're welcome. We're going to be making our dessert, banana bread. Did Cassie tell you?"

Tanner's gaze darted to Cassie with a clear SOS message. "Mom, I don't think Tanner has time—"

"Nonsense. There's nothing waiting for him back at that big old empty house. We'll just clear off the table and get started. We'll make the banana bread first so it can cool while we're making the others."

Cassie sent him a look that said, "I tried."

"And Tanner, I want you to know you have a standing invitation to come for dinner and bread making on Thursdays."

"Thank you, Mrs. Lei—" Her raised eyebrows reprimanded him. "I mean, Diane."

Cassie harrumphed. "She should be thanking *you,* Tanner. Believe me, she makes out on the deal. Cheap labor."

"Now, Cassie, don't scare him off. Honestly, Tanner, it'll be fun. Just wait and see."

Tanner had assumed that a word from Cassie would pave the way for his quick exit. What had he gotten himself into?

An hour later found Tanner at the kitchen counter, covered with flour and kneading dough. And enjoying it, which was even more surprising, since he'd never even attempted cut-and-bake cookies from the grocery store. The company, though, probably had more to do with his enjoyment than the process itself.

His standing invitation to dinner and bread making for every Thursday was too foreign of a notion to comprehend.

He'd experienced another odd sensation while measuring vanilla for the banana bread. The now familiar scent made him wonder about his grandmother that he'd never known, a woman so special that for years after her death her husband had simmered the spice on the stove to feel close to her.

Tanner's gaze had instinctively sought out Cassie and found her smiling at him, leaving no doubt their thoughts were the same.

He'd known Cassie a short time, and yet at that moment it felt as if they were old lovers with a long past, shared secrets and inside jokes. The sensation was scary and exhilarating at the same time. Maybe the next twenty-three days would pass by quicker, and be more enjoyable, than he'd thought.

"That's right, Tanner, knead the dough with the heels of your hands, then fold it over. And don't be afraid to add flour if it's too sticky."

Tanner leaned into the job, using the weight of his upper body to put pressure on the dough the way Diane had instructed. "How do you know when to stop?" he asked, although he wasn't concerned with the answer. Kneading dough proved as therapeutic as working with wood, just in a different way, and he couldn't wait to get to the part where he got to punch in the dough. Meanwhile, his stomach growled at the prospect of tasting the banana bread that cooled on a nearby rack.

"About five minutes. The dough will look smooth

and bounce back after you press it in with your fingertip.''

"Add flour *if* you need it,'' Cassie said dryly as she stirred eggs and water in a bowl, a mixture that supposedly made the crust shiny if brushed on the loaf before baking. "*About* no more than five minutes,'' she continued. "That's what makes me crazy about baking bread. There are no absolutes. Humidity or even the age of the yeast can throw off the numbers. Give me hanging wallpaper any day. The numbers don't change each time you measure.''

Flour dusted the tip of Cassie's nose and Tanner battled with the urge to reach across the table and wipe it away with his finger. He knew her skin was soft....

Diane leaned toward Tanner. "You know how animals can sense if you're afraid?'' she asked out of the corner of her mouth, as if Cassie couldn't hear.

Tanner nodded, curious where Diane was headed with such an odd remark.

"Well, I think yeast can sense when you're afraid and it just won't cooperate if you are.''

"That's quite a theory,'' he said, careful not to look Cassie's way or risk breaking into laughter.

"You can't be great at everything,'' Cassie countered. "I accept that my talents lie elsewhere.''

With a will of its own, his gaze drifted in her direction. He already knew of at least one of her talents—she was one heck of a kisser. Something told him that she had many more.

"You know, Mom, they have machines that make bread,'' Cassie quipped, relegated to stirring the mixture once the ingredients had been added to a large bowl.

"I know, dear. But the loaves are a funny shape and it's just not the same."

"If people are hungry, they don't care what it looks like."

Diane laughed. "Tanner, would you believe we've been having a variation of this same conversation since Cassie was old enough to speak her mind?"

Tanner grinned at Cassie. "I believe it." He could easily picture her as a young girl in pigtails, determined to change tradition.

"I sure miss the old days." Diane sighed. "Every Thursday the entire family gathered at my mom's house to break bread. Even the men. Of course, they were too impatient to mess with yeast and made the quick breads like banana or pumpkin."

Tanner couldn't imagine such a tradition-filled childhood. A truck driver, his dad had been gone a lot; his mom was always there, but with money so tight, she was usually busy with the ironing and alterations she took in for extra cash; she had little time or energy left over for much else.

"Now, Jill, she loves working in the kitchen," Diane continued. "It's too bad she—"

"Mom, can you hand me a paper towel?" Cassie interrupted. "My hands are yucky."

Her mom ripped off a square and handed it to her. "At least you don't lick your fingers anymore. Tanner, you wouldn't believe how many batches were ruined because I'd catch her licking her fingers or the spoon before she was done."

Cassie didn't mind the teasing since it helped direct the conversation away from her sister. Jill wouldn't appreciate a stranger knowing all the details of her failed marriage, a subject she assumed the whole town talked about.

"Tanner, you're making a big mistake, you know," Cassie said, intent on keeping the subject off of her sister. "You're doing such a great job, if you don't watch out, you'll find yourself here every Thursday."

Diane smiled. "That would be wonderful! Lord knows you're a wet blanket about the whole thing. I just don't understand how someone who is so exact in measuring wallpaper or fabric, can be so off when it comes to baking. Why, Tanner, one time…"

Cassie sighed and settled in to hear the worn-out story of her miserable attempt at making "no fuss fudge" in the microwave. The darn stuff had blown up and coated the walls of the oven with chocolate goo. Could happen to anybody.

Cassie had opened all the kitchen windows because of the fumes. She worked at a brisk pace to get the second coat of enamel on the woodwork before she lost all natural light at Fairfax House. She was exhausted, having stayed at her mom's last night much later than usual, but the time had been well spent.

Although Tanner had claimed it wasn't a big deal that he'd lost all pictures of his family, Cassie didn't believe him. He was just being a guy.

After going through countless scrapbooks, she had finally found a picture of Tanner's mother, and then chose one out of the many photos of his father.

Cassie would find the perfect double frame, have the pictures matted and surprise Tanner with the gift.

She had deemed the evening a huge success in

many ways. Not only had her mother enjoyed the walk down memory lane, but Tanner had been charmed by his hostess, as expected, and had seemed reluctant to leave.

Mr. Howard and the boys had continued to rave over Tanner's carpentry and instructional skills. Things were beginning to look up. She dared to hope she could blow off the appointment with the loan officer at the bank.

Cassie heard whistling and a chugging engine. She peeked out the window and saw Tanner hop out of Mr. Howard's ancient pickup. Where was Tanner's truck?

She cleaned up her painting mess while she waited for Tanner to appear. Within minutes the kitchen door slammed shut. "Hi, Cassie."

She glanced up. Did he ever look good. There was something sexy about a man who worked with his hands, unafraid to sweat or get dirty. He exuded maleness, made her fantasize of being swept up in his strong arms and carried off to a warm shower....

"Is something wrong?"

Oh, yes. She blinked to clear the images from her mind. "Um, no. I was just finishing up when I heard Mr. Howard's truck. What happened to yours?"

"The blasted thing wouldn't start. Before I knew it, some guy named Sam had come by and towed it to his garage. Said he'd order whatever was needed and bill me. I tried to give him a credit card and he said no Fairfax would pay up front as long as he was running things. Then Mr. Howard insisted on being my taxi to and from the festival site for as long as I needed."

Tanner raked his hand through his thick, black

hair, leaving it attractively ruffled. "This whole town is nuts. They don't know me from Adam."

Why did he have to be so adorable when he was flustered? Focus, Cassie, focus. "Tanner, they knew your family, you're helping Pete and the boys. What more do they need to know?"

"I'm not helping with the festival because I'm a nice guy, I'm helping because I owe Pete. There's a difference."

She shrugged. "Whether you like it or not, the town has accepted you."

Tanner shook his head. "Unreal."

"Listen, this is your last chance to have a say in the wallpaper. Tomorrow morning I'm going to mud and sand the walls, and I'll start hanging on Monday. Are you sure you don't want to choose the paper yourself?"

"Positive." He tossed his keys on the table.

Not exactly the answer she'd hoped for, but his indifference toward the wallpaper didn't take away the gains made at dinner. "I'll see you tomorrow, then."

"Actually, before my truck broke down, I had planned on asking you to dinner tonight, if you didn't already have plans."

"You were?" Cassie was more than a little surprised by the invitation. Last night must've gone even better than imagined.

He nodded. "Sort of a thank you for the great time at your mom's, and to celebrate wrapping up the job here. I should get my truck back by Tuesday. We can plan something for then, or I could rent a car tomorrow."

She wasn't about to pass up the chance to build

on the goodwill created the night before. "I wouldn't waste money on a car in such a small town. In fact, if you're serious about dinner tonight, I know of a great place, and it's within walking distance. Very casual. Shorts and sandals."

"I was thinking of something a little nicer, but if this is where you want to go, it's fine with me. What time?"

"I'll meet you out front in an hour."

"These are the best wingdings I've ever had," Tanner said as he licked the barbeque sauce from his fingers and grabbed another chicken wing. "Of course, I didn't even know what a wingding was until now."

"I wish you could've seen your face when you realized we were going to Camp's for dinner. It was priceless."

"Just the effect you were going for?"

"Right."

At first, Tanner had been put off by the idea of spending any time at a place that made him remember things he'd rather forget. He already had to clamp down on the memories each day he worked at the festival site. But to actually sit at a red table under a red-and-white umbrella just like before? What excuse would he have given Cassie, though?

"Hello, Tanner. Enjoying your meal?"

Tanner glanced up to find a black Lexus parked several feet away, the windows down. The expensive car looked out of place on the gravel. "You bet, Mr. Samuels." Tanner leaned toward Cassie. "A lawyer at a drive-in?"

"Even lawyers have to eat. And like you said, Pete's wingdings are the best."

"I guess so. What is in the sauce? It's great." Tanner finished the last chicken wing, then used a packaged moist wipe to clean his hands.

"Pete's secret recipe. I don't think even his wife knows. Mardell is sweet, but she loves to talk."

"Hey, Cassie, I finally decided on the color of paint. I'll call you on Monday."

Cassie smiled and waved at a woman in a gray Passport. "Okay, Mrs. Goodman."

Tanner couldn't get over how the whole town seemed like a big family.

"Ready for dessert?" Cassie asked. "They have great sundaes."

"Do they still have the dipped cones?"

"Sure, but how did you know...? Oh, that's right. You said you'd been here once before." She stood. "Our waitress looks swamped, so I'm just going to order at the window. Dessert is my treat, since you paid for dinner." Without waiting for his reply, Cassie headed for the order window.

Tanner stretched his legs while he appreciated the sight of Cassie's shapely backside outlined in black denim. The shorts were cuffed, several inches above the knees. She wore a sleeveless white blouse tied at the waist. And of course, something on her head, a white combination visor-baseball cap that tied in back.

The look was casual, comfortable and revealed an inner confidence. Some women just tried too hard, would've rolled the shorts up too high, or tied the shirt to show off their stomach.

Now, if Cassie had been dressing just for him, that

was a different story. In private, the hat would go first. He wanted to see her hair wild and free. Then, he'd waste no time tugging at the knot on Cassie's shirt...

"I got you a large," Cassie said, which effectively put the freeze on his daydreaming. Just as well.

"Hope you can handle it," she baited.

He knew what he'd like to handle, and it would definitely involve licking something other than ice cream. Suddenly, he was no longer comfortable in his shorts and T-shirt, but very, very hot. He struggled to get his mind out of the gutter. Cassie was different than the women he usually dated, not someone to treat casually. "I'll give it a shot." He gestured at her sundae. "What is *that?*" The concoction looked as if everything but the kitchen sink had been dumped in the bowl.

"I invented this work of art when I worked here as a kid. I dubbed it the 'banana split blitz.' A little bit of everything."

"You used to work here?" He took several licks of the cone as he turned it to catch any drips. The brittle chocolate coating split into small pieces to mix with the soft vanilla ice cream. Just as he remembered, but a little more manageable now.

"Sure. Most kids around here have, at some point. Pete and Mardell could never have kids of their own, so they pretty much adopt all kids. If you need a sponsor for your youth team, call Pete. If you need a job, call Pete."

"And if you need extra credit for shop class," Tanner interjected, "call Pete."

Cassie nodded. "I'm glad his injury wasn't too serious. He's a great guy."

"I know." For some reason, Tanner wanted to talk about that day, more than twenty years ago. Cassie was just easy to talk to, he guessed. "I met Pete when I was five, the day my dad took me to see my grandfather for the first and only time. They had this huge fight, about me. My dad stopped here to get me an ice-cream cone to calm me down."

Cassie had stopped eating, her total attention on him. Compassion filled her dark green eyes.

"I could tell my dad and Pete had been buddies. He was kind to me, but not condescending. Told me a story that probably had a lesson in it somewhere, but I was too young to understand."

She nodded. "That's Pete. He's known for his stories. If you take the time to figure them out, he's usually right." She took another bite of her sundae, licking the spoon clean after every taste. "So that's why you wanted to help Pete?"

"Sure. Even though I didn't understand all that he was telling me, he obviously cared. He could've ignored me or talked down to me. I know it meant a lot to my dad, too. Pete knew my grandfather, knew what had happened before."

"That's one of the nice things about a small town. Everyone knows everything about everyone. Of course, that can be a bad thing, too, because there are no secrets."

The conversation had become much too maudlin. "So, what's the worst thing you ever did that the whole town talked about?"

She laughed and shook her head.

"I can always ask your mom."

"No way. She'd probably tell you something ten times more embarrassing. Let me think."

Cassie's face scrunched up in concentration. He was sorely tempted to kiss her pert nose. "I guess it'd be when I got caught drag racing out on 189."

Tanner nearly dropped his cone. "You?"

"What? Because I'm a girl?"

"Well, yeah."

"That's what got the whole thing started. I was buddies with Todd and Jerry and when I heard they were challenging kids from a rival school to a drag race, and they hadn't included me, I was furious. So I borrowed Mr. Frank's Thunderbird, but didn't tell him why, and showed up for the race. Boy, did I think I was hot stuff."

Tanner could picture Cassie charging off to prove a point. "Weren't you afraid of something happening to the car?"

"At sixteen? Come on. I was all hormones and false bravado. Thank heavens nothing did happen, since the police got wind of the race. The town talked about it for months."

"What happened to you?"

"Mr. Frank verified he'd given me permission to borrow the car, but not for that reason. It was my first offense, so I got off with a stern warning. I was grounded for two months, no driving. But the worst thing was how I'd disappointed Mr. Frank. It was a long time before he trusted me, and that just about killed me. But, he eventually forgave me, even let me take the car out for spin every now and then."

So, the old man could forgive some things. Too bad he couldn't have done the same for his own son.

Chapter Seven

Tanner stood and threw the mushy remains of his cone in the trash. "Am I ever full. The walk back will feel good. Are you ready to go?"

"Oh, no you don't." She walked over to him and blocked his way, her hands on her hips. "I've spilled my guts. Now it's your turn. Fess up, or we'll be here all night."

He raised his hands in surrender. "Okay, okay. I guess that's only fair," he said, and motioned for her to join him as he began walking. "My junior year in high school I skipped all day to go to an auto show in Dallas. Me and my buddy, Steve, thought we had all the bases covered, that there was no way we'd get caught. And we would've made it, too, except that Steve's dad had snuck away from work to do the same thing and we were busted. Of course, the dad was, too, especially because he didn't make us leave right away."

"You're kidding, right?"

Her stride matched his, a rarity, and he found himself relaxing more and more. A few times he had almost reached for her hand, it had seemed the natural thing to do, but he fought the impulse. This wasn't a date. "No kidding. It was too long of a drive to go all that way for nothing. Our story was that he didn't see us until later. And I didn't see anything but the four walls of my room for a long time. It was worth it, though. We saw some awesome cars that day."

Cassie shook her head. "I guess we weren't angels, but we weren't that bad, either. I'm just now hearing about some of my mom's escapades. It's so weird thinking of your parents as teenagers, getting into trouble, going out on dates."

She stopped abruptly and playfully punched at his right arm, her green eyes wide. "Do you realize that if our parents hadn't broken up we could be brother and sister?"

The possibility left him stunned, speechless.

Laughter tumbled from Cassie's mouth. "Thank heavens for Martha Billings. To this day, I'm not sure Mom has forgiven her for stealing your dad away."

Relief swept over Tanner and he chuckled, grateful he could relive the fantastic kiss in the dark closet with a clear conscience. "If I ever meet Martha, I'll be sure and thank her."

Cassie began to walk again and he fell into step beside her, unable to recall ever feeling so aware of a woman before, yet comfortable. He wondered if he dared ask the question burning in his mind, then decided to go for it. "Can I ask you a personal question?"

A skeptical expression crossed her face. "Depends. What is it?"

"There doesn't seem to be a guy in your life and I can't for the life of me imagine why."

Her eyes widened. "That came out of nowhere. But thanks, I think."

"Forget it."

"No, it's all right. I was involved with someone for about a year and we broke up a couple of months ago. Let's just say I don't have trouble meeting men, and when I do get involved, it usually lasts for a while. But I know what I'm looking for, so I don't waste my time on a guy after I find out we don't want the same things."

From the beginning he'd known they were wrong for each other, and she'd just confirmed it. She wanted him to stay and live at Fairfax House; he planned to leave as soon as possible.

"What about you, Tanner? Anyone special waiting back in Tyler?"

He shook his head. "I'm never in one place for very long. But that's the way I like it."

She laughed nervously. "This is getting way too serious." She pointed to a massive pond on her right. Ducks idly skimmed the surface and bobbed for bread crumbs being tossed by a handful of kids. "That's Miller's Pond. Did you know Kate Bishop, my sister and I are the human sled champs of '88?"

"Human sled?"

Cassie threw him a look of disbelief. "I forgot. I'm talking to a Texan. The pond freezes in the winter and we ice-skate and play all sorts of games, like crack the whip or tag. A human sled is where one person squats down and puts her hands on top of the skates of the person standing behind her, and that person bends over and puts her hands on the other's knees. Then the third person pushes. It's a blast.''

Although the sun had set, the temperature still hovered around the mideighties, so Tanner had a difficult time picturing the pond a sheet of ice.

''And on days it's real cold, someone makes a fire so we can huddle around it and get warm.''

Now *that* was something he could imagine. The first time he laid eyes on Cassie, she had him thinking about campfires, hayrides and walks in the rain, things he knew nothing about.

He'd never lived anywhere with a real change of seasons. In Texas, if you blinked, you missed spring and fall, and winter usually proved fleeting and fairly mild.

What would it be like to live in a place such as New Haven, where the seasons changed, but the faces around you didn't?

Before long they reached Fairfax House and he was surprised to find he wished the night didn't have to end.

Cassie couldn't recall ever feeling so unnerved during a goodbye on a nondate. She didn't drink coffee so late, and both of them had to get up early in the morning, yet her mind raced for reasons to prolong the evening, and came up empty. ''Thanks for dinner. It was great.''

''And thank *you* for dessert. Next time I'll have to try one of your blitzes.''

Next time. Such sweet, unexpected words. Tanner usually hid behind walls, but the last two nights she had observed a relaxed, funny, warm side of him that proved very attractive. How long would this new-and-improved version of him last?

"I'll walk you to your door."

"No need. I'm just across the street." Cassie reminded herself again that this wasn't a date, and she didn't want to risk an awkward moment of "will he or won't he kiss me?" Not when she already knew how his kisses burned all thought and logic from her mind. "I'll be by in the morning around nine, and after I'm done here, I'll help out at the site. Georgie, Mike and Danny said they'd drop by at some point, and I'm sure there will be others, too."

"Why not invite the whole town?"

She grinned. "It could happen." Tonight was proof that anything could happen—she and Tanner had shared a little bit of themselves with each other, and hadn't argued once.

Cassie left Pete's house around one o'clock Saturday afternoon after repeated assurance she would report back on the progress next door at the festival site. She had found him on crutches, cranky as a baby with colic.

She refused to let anything spoil her good mood, though. The sun was shining, and the weatherman had predicted the rain would hold off until tomorrow, so lots of work would get done on the stage. Even better than that, though, was the tingle of pleasure which surfaced when she recalled the evening spent with Tanner.

Over wingdings and ice cream he had let down his guard, revealed some of his past. He was beginning to trust her.

When she had checked her phone messages that

night, her mother had called with news of her gift of cookie presses from Tanner. The delight in her voice had made Cassie smile. And just as Fairfax House was becoming more open and warm, so was its owner.

Things really were looking up.

"Miss Cassie, Miss Cassie, I scored another goal yesterday!" Emily yelled as she ran toward Cassie.

Cassie swooped the little girl up into her arms and kissed her on the cheek. "Good job, pumpkin. Where's your mom?"

"She's over talking to that tall man over there."

Cassie followed the direction of Emily's chubby finger and found Tanner dressed in his usual T-shirt, worn jeans and boots. But the way he filled out his clothes proved anything but ordinary. His tan had deepened from working under the relentless July sun and provided a great backdrop for the scarce, genuine smile currently on his face.

She had wanted to thank him for the thoughtful gift to her mother first thing this morning, but the site had been too crowded. When she had arrived at nine, the three boys, Georgie, Danny, Mike, and a handful of others were already at work. And of course, Tanner.

He never hesitated to get dirty with the rest of them. At the same time he kept a sharp eye on all that went on around him. He was quick to praise the boys and she could see they had gained more confidence.

Most of the two-by-tens had been cut to specification earlier that week. Today's agenda involved using the precut wood to make sixteen-by-thirty-two

sections that would eventually be screwed together
and bolted to cinder blocks to create the stage floor.

The crew was now obviously on a break. Georgie,
Mike and Danny huddled around Tanner and all
seemed in high spirits. Her heart warmed at the sight
of Tanner so at ease with her subcontractors, who
were like family. Georgie, her best friend, was the
older sister she never had. Twenty-six and a single
mom, she had an abundance of compassion and
strength. She was also the best darned painter and
wallpaper hanger in the county.

Mike, three years older and married with two kids,
was such an exceptional plumber and general han-
dyman that people waited until he was free rather
than call someone else.

Two years younger and full of fire, Danny had a
true gift for working with wood. He also had a passion for race car driving, a hobby that ate up most
of his money. Cassie worried about him, but tried
not to nag.

With a will of its own, her gaze returned to Tanner, a man who constantly surprised her. What else
would she discover about him if he decided to stay?
She couldn't deny how her heart quickened at the
thought, but she wasn't the type to act recklessly.
Time would tell.

Emily wiggled out of Cassie's arms and ran to her
mother. Cassie forced her mind off Tanner and the
questionable future and onto a mystery she *knew* she
could solve—what had they all found so amusing?
She approached the group.

"It was our first job, right?" Mike said, obviously
unaware of her arrival. "Cassie skimped on money
for a ladder and it was junk, but she wouldn't listen

to us. I thought her eyes were going to pop out of her head when that ferret dashed across the ledge in front of her at old man Warner's house.''

Danny shook his head and laughed. ''Oh, man. I have never seen her so freaked out. The ladder was moving all over the place because she was shaking so bad. We were all laughing so hard, we could barely hold the ladder still.''

''Tanner, you should have seen her,'' Georgie chimed in. ''It was so hilarious. But, she's never bought a cheap ladder since.''

''You people need some new material,'' Cassie chided, determined to hide the mixed emotions Tanner stirred inside her. ''That story is so old.''

Tanner grinned. ''Not to me.''

Relief swept through her that he continued to act comfortably around her. Until that moment, she hadn't realized that she'd feared he would have regrets about letting his guard down last night. He had changed moods on her before.

''I see how it is.'' She struggled to keep her tone casual; she didn't want her friends to suspect the effect Tanner had on her. It was bad enough that *she* knew how eagerly she had returned his kiss in the dark closet, and how absolutely crestfallen she had felt when he had stopped. ''Just remember, I have dirt on every one of you.'' She turned to Tanner. ''Rule number three in a small town, Tanner—what goes around comes around, only quicker.''

Cassie felt a tug on her hand. ''Miss Cassie, you promised me a ice-cream cone.''

''Emily! That's rude.''

''No, she's right, Georgie. One goal, one cone, coming up.''

"Wait for me, then," Georgie said. "I don't want her to get the biggest one." She turned to Tanner and shook his hand. "It was great meeting you, and I think it's wonderful how you're helping out Pete and the boys. And remember, it's not just women who are allowed to change their minds. We'd love to have you stay and keep Fairfax House in the family." She turned to her daughter. "Emily, say goodbye to Mr. Fairfax."

She stayed at Cassie's side and waved her pudgy little hand. "Bye Mr. Fairfax."

He smiled and waved back. "Goodbye, Emily. Stay tough on the soccer field."

Emily giggled. "I will."

"Wow. That man's smile could melt Miller's Pond in the middle of winter," Georgie said as soon as Tanner was out of earshot.

Yeah, Cassie silently agreed, but his kisses could turn that same pond into a sauna. No, she had to forget. At least until she knew for sure what his future plans were for Fairfax House, for himself.

Georgie fanned herself with one hand. "Now I know why you're avoiding Greg. The poor guy asks about you every time I see him at the mailboxes. I keep telling him you're really busy, but now that I know your latest project is such a hunk—"

"I *am* busy, and there isn't any point in going out with your neighbor again. He's moving to Columbus in the fall and has no plans to move back."

"What's a hunk, Mommy?"

"Never mind, Emily. Miss Cassie and I are talking."

"And Tanner is not a project, Georgie."

"Might as well be one. From what little you've

told me, he wants to sell Fairfax House and you promised his grandfather you'd try to change his mind. If that's not a job, I don't know what is.''

"I was pretty concerned at first, but I think he's coming around.''

"Does this positive outlook have anything to do with the sparks flying between you two? You weren't this rattled when you were going with Wayne.'' Georgie hooked her arm through Cassie's as they walked toward the diner. "I'm your best friend, Cas. Come on, you can tell me.''

Sparks sounded too mild. More like an electrical storm. What she had experienced with Wayne paled in comparison on every level. When it had become obvious he wanted her, but nothing to do with her family, she'd made the only choice possible and had no regrets.

She wouldn't give up on looking for Mr. Right, though. Someday, she'd find a man who not only loved her but New Haven and her family, who wanted to be her partner in every way possible. "Okay, so there's some chemistry between us. But that's all. We're not pursuing it.''

"But?''

"But I can't deny that if I knew for sure that he was staying, I'd probably want to pursue it. Bad.''

"Oh, boy. Are you still going to meet with the bank next week? I mean, you'd have to put everything on the line in order to make it happen.''

"I guess I should, just to cover my bases. I can't stand the thought of that beautiful house being turned into offices. Tell me again you think I could make a go of turning it into a boardinghouse if it comes down to that.''

"I really do. Housing is tough to find around here. Shoot, I'll be the first in line if you buy the house. I think it would be fun, and Emily would love the huge backyard."

"Mooom. Can I pleeease have my ice cream now?"

Tanner observed Cassie, Georgie and Emily pass the old oak on their way to the drive-in. He was amazed by how Cassie and her crew acted like family, right down to the teasing so common among brothers and sisters.

An only child whose dad had been gone a lot, Tanner hadn't grown up around lots of people or noise. Later, he realized he was accepted solely based on what someone wanted from him. As an employee, he knew the boss expected so many hours of hard work a week from him.

Now, as a boss, employees treated him with a certain respect because he signed their paychecks. He might have a couple of beers with the guys after work, but they weren't real friends. No one hung around long enough for that, including him.

For some reason, Cassie and her crew seemed eager to include him in their "family." Danny had offered to give a tour of the race track, Mike had invited him to a cookout with his wife and kids and Georgie let him know the date of Emily's next game, in case he wanted to come. Heck, the whole town acted eager to adopt him, had even asked him to lead their parade.

And Cassie... What did she want to give him? Certainly not what he really wanted, if he was honest with himself. As if they had mutually agreed, the tone last night had remained light.

No holding hands, no stolen kisses, even though he'd been tempted numerous times. She had made a fast-food dinner and a walk more enjoyable than a meal at a five-star restaurant and limo ride, and he couldn't seem to get enough of her.

A part of him wished that first kiss in the dark closet had never ended. The chemistry between them was like nothing he'd ever experienced before. He ached to know if she made love with the same drawn-out passion she applied to eating a favorite dessert.

He'd never know. No strings, he reminded himself. He didn't want any ties to New Haven, and she was as rooted to the town as that huge oak tree behind the drive-in.

Except for last night, all Cassie's interest seemed centered on convincing him that Fairfax House was his home and that he shouldn't sell. Why that remained so important to her, he had no idea. He still had three weeks to find out, though.

He glanced at his watch. Time to get back to work.

"Hey, Mr. Fairfax, I mean, Tanner." Cory ran toward Tanner. "Are you coming tonight?"

"Coming where?"

"The jazz concert. In the park. They usually have all adults, but our band teacher convinced them to let a group of us do a set. I play trumpet. Ben plays the sax. He told me not to bother you, but I figured, why not?"

"That's great, Cory, but I—"

Cory's shoulders slumped. "It's okay. Not everyone likes jazz."

Tanner was floored that boys he'd just met five days ago, including Ben, who tried too hard to act tough, cared one way or the other if he came. But they obviously did, and he couldn't let them down. Besides, his calendar wasn't exactly full these days. "I love jazz. I just need to know where and when."

Tanner made sure he had locked the house before he left on his walk down Main Street to the park. He had been assured he'd have the part needed for his truck by Monday. Since he was technically on vacation, and the town was so small, he just hadn't bothered to check into a car rental.

Besides, walking stretched his legs. The clean air held just the slightest hint of rain, which the weatherman promised would hold off until tomorrow.

With so little traffic, he could hear music blaring from open windows, along with a strange, shrill sound that reminded him of the cicadas back home.

"Young Fairfax, you want a lift?" Mr. Howard called out from his rattling truck. He never could remember Tanner's name.

"No, thanks. I'm just going to the park."

"Okay. See you there."

Tanner's leisurely pace allowed time to admire the unique architecture of the houses along the way. Some resembled Victorian, gingerbreadlike houses, with sections painted different colors. Others boasted a Colonial flavor. Lots of history. So many stories. No doubt Cassie knew them all.

Cassie. Would she be there tonight?

No. He wouldn't give her another thought. Last night proved she was different from the other women he could just date. He'd never opened up about the past, about personal things, to anyone before.

Cassie was dangerous to his peace of mind.

The sound of instruments warming up and the hum of a chatty crowd signaled the park was near. As he got closer, people stopped him to say, "hello," or ask questions about Pete's injuries, or the progress of the festival site. Cory and Allen's parents had thanked him for stepping in to help their boys. Somehow, he wasn't surprised that no one had approached him on Ben's behalf.

A blanket of acceptance enveloped Tanner, made it easy to smile and join in the small talk.

He gave a thumbs-up to Cory, who squirmed in dark slacks, white shirt and tie, but managed a weak grin in Tanner's direction before turning his attention back to his sheet music. Ben had simply nodded, but he was just better at hiding his feelings, Tanner guessed.

The concert began. The crowd gathered on benches or blankets. Old people with canes sat next to babies in strollers. The scene reminded him of a Norman Rockwell painting.

The band was excellent, but Tanner had something—or someone—else on his mind.

He told himself he wasn't looking for anyone in particular as he scanned the crowd, when he knew deep down he hoped to find a certain woman who would grab his attention whether or not she wore a hat.

"I was hoping I'd find you here."

Tanner turned around to find Cassie, dressed in a sleeveless blouse the same color as her green eyes.

A short flowered skirt revealed legs that seemed to go on forever. He swallowed hard. "You were?"

She nodded. "I wanted you to know how much Mom loved her cookie presses, if you haven't heard from her yet. But you didn't have to do anything. It was just dinner, and we even put you to work afterward."

Cassie was wrong. The night had involved so much more than a meal. He hadn't felt part of a family in so long and they had made it easy for him.

He gestured toward the stage. "Do you know anyone up there but Cory and Ben? Or is that a stupid question?"

She grinned. "Very. Although sometimes they'll bring in a ringer. People go crazy trying to figure out who they are, who they're related to, or where they're from. One time Jill invited a guy friend from college to sit in for a neighbor who had to go out of town. You should have heard the speculation over who he was, where he was from. Jill made it worse by making up these horrible stories about him. We laughed over that for months." Cassie sighed. "I sure miss her craziness."

"Is Jill sick or something? You and your mom sound so sad whenever you mention her."

"No. She's reeling from a nasty divorce. I swear I will never let what happened to her happen to me." Cassie's eyes widened, as if surprised she had spoken out loud. "Forget what I said. It's family business. I shouldn't have said anything."

"Divorce happens, Cassie. There aren't any guarantees."

"No, but I saw the result of two people spending all their time chasing after separate dreams. I think half the people in this town are divorced. When I settle down, it's going to be with someone who wants to work together, too. That way we'd both be going in the same direction."

Tanner felt as if he'd been sucker punched. Even though he'd never seriously considered getting involved with Cassie, her revelation firmly closed the door on the possibility. He'd been on his own too long to consider being around someone twenty-four hours a day, seven days a week. "Sounds more like being suffocated, to me."

Cassie shrugged and averted her gaze over his left shoulder. "To each his own. My mom lost the love of her life way too early, and missed out on time together because of my dad's typical seventy-hour week. Your grandfather, whatever you might say bad about him, truly loved your grandmother, and lost her too soon. And I'm sure your parents expected to grow old together. So much precious time was spent apart."

Tanner had expected Cassie to act stunned or disappointed over his dig on togetherness, instead of her nonchalant shrug. He should be relieved. No, he *was* relieved, dammit. "My dad was gone a lot, but I don't think they had much choice about being apart. They loved each other and that was what mattered."

"Not everyone is so lucky. I'm not taking any chances."

Tanner didn't even attempt to respond to such a foreign belief. Whether the cause was from divorce or death, being left alone was devastating. He had no desire to go through the hell of losing someone close again.

As the band reached a crescendo of a rousing number, the shrill noise he'd heard earlier returned, at five times the volume.

"Isn't it amazing how loud the katydids are?" Cassie asked. "You'd think they were in competition with the band."

He latched onto the distraction. "So, that's what they're called. In Texas, we have cicadas. But from the looks of that dark cloud, the band has more than noisy bugs to worry about. So much for believing the weatherman."

Raindrops splattered from the sky. The band headed for a small, covered pavilion while the crowd made a mass exodus from the park.

Cassie spun slowly in a circle, arms out wide, a smile on her rain-kissed face. "Doesn't this feel wonderful?" Her eyes sparkled. "Why is it that when you grow up, you're not supposed to want to play in the rain or stomp in mud puddles?"

Tanner knew all about the desire to do something he shouldn't. He stared at Cassie, so completely absorbed in the pleasure of the moment. She took his breath away. He was reminded of the first day they met, when the sight of her had made him think crazy, mushy thoughts. "I'll walk you to your van. Where did you park?"

"I didn't. It was such a pretty night I decided to walk. Wait, your truck is still in the shop. Did you walk, too?"

He nodded grimly and scoped the park, only to find a handful of people left. Trouble.

Cassie chuckled and put a hand on his arm. "What's wrong, Tanner. You're not afraid of a little rain, are you?"

Her touch created more heat than a lightning bolt from the sky. Rain was the last thing he feared.

"Come on," she urged. "Let's enjoy this excuse to play in the rain." She took his hand and began to walk. He followed her lead and a sense of contentment washed over him.

Along the way, she stomped in puddles and challenged him to a splashing contest; she revealed the personal stories behind the more interesting houses.

Her wet clothes clung to her body and outlined every tempting curve. Her smile and sense of fun proved contagious. He had laughed so much during the last twenty minutes his side ached; he never wanted the walk to end.

He glanced up and saw Fairfax House, just a block away. Disappointment weighed him down and slowed his feet.

Cassie watched the smile fade from Tanner's face and wondered what could have changed his mood so quickly. She'd have none of it, the day was too perfect. She hopped up onto brick edging near the sidewalk and held on to his shoulder for balance while she walked.

A branch of a nearby tree made her pause, but instead of ducking underneath, she shook it and gave him another shower.

"Hey. You're not playing fair," he complained as he pulled her down to the sidewalk.

The sparkle reappeared in his eyes. "Like you were fair during the splashing contest. Your boots are the size of small boats. Talk about unfair advantage."

She stood facing him, mere inches away; she felt

her chest rising and falling with each breath as she waited for the friendly argument to continue.

He gently gripped her shoulders and pulled her against him. She knew he was going to kiss her, but anticipation clouded all logic and reason for resisting. Just as the parched earth had surely welcomed the refreshing summer rain, she greedily accepted his kisses, his touch.

With obvious reluctance, he pulled away and rested his forehead against hers. "You make me crazy," he murmured.

She struggled to find her voice. "I do?"

"From the moment I first laid eyes on you," he said, as he outlined her swollen mouth with his fingers. "One look, and I was picturing the two of us taking walks in the rain, going on hayrides and sharing a campfire. And it's crazy, because I've never done any of those things."

She smiled, determined to keep the mood light. "Of course not. What would a Texan know about huddling under a blanket on a crisp fall night during a hayride? Or warming yourself by campfire on a cold winter day?"

"Well, we might not know about cold, but we Texans sure know about heat," he murmured, and covered her face with light kisses.

She closed her eyes under the tender assault and sighed. "You're not playing fair, again."

"I know. And I promised myself I wouldn't let this happen. It's not fair to you. I leave in three weeks."

The reminder of time running out forced her eyes

open. She had planned to take things slow, but what if she waited too long to say how she really felt, and he mistook her silence as a sign she didn't care if he remained or left town? "Stay, Tanner."

Chapter Eight

Tanner froze. "What?"

"We'll do all those things, Tanner. Hayrides and campfires. You should see this town in the wintertime. It's beautiful."

"You know I can't do that."

"Why not?"

He stepped back and thrust his hands in his pockets. "My life is back in Tyler."

Cassie braced herself to give the most convincing argument of her life. "Is it really? You admitted you don't have a home in Tyler, just an apartment where you pick up mail and clean clothes. You move around constantly with your work, so it must be hard to make friends. In the short time you've been here, you've already made friends. Why won't you even consider keeping your family home?"

"Why is it so important to you? Ever since I arrived, you've been trying to make me care about the house and town. What's in it for you? Did my grandfather pay you off, hoping you would try to convince me to stay and save his precious house?"

"That's a despicable thing to say."

"We are talking about my grandfather. I wouldn't put anything past him. It's not as if I'd blame you if you had made some sort of deal. It's only sweeter if he wasted money on a losing proposition. Don't worry though, you did your job."

Cassie curled her hands into fists and fought the urge to slap the smug expression off his face. "You know, when I first read about you and how you were on the move a lot, no close friends, no long-term relationships, I wanted to help—"

Anger flashed in Tanner's gaze. "What do you mean, you read about me? How would you know about my personal life?"

Cassie felt the color drain from her face. She'd wanted to hurt him for making such a horrible accusation about her, and had only made matters worse. "Tanner, listen—"

"What kind of game are you playing? Have you had someone checking up on me?"

She had always intended to tell Tanner about the report, but not now, not when he was already so angry. "Of course not. It was your grandfather. He was worried about you, so he hired an investigator to find out if you needed anything, but he never interfered. I didn't want to tell you before, because I knew you would misinterpret his reasons."

"You're the one who's confused, if you think my grandfather was anything but a power-hungry, self-serving jerk."

"People can change. Read his letter, please, before

you make a final decision about the house or about leaving.''

"The decision is already made. And if you're serious about bidding on Fairfax House, you'd better get moving. You've got twenty-one days.''

"You bet I'm serious. You'll have my bid by Friday.''

"Bless you, Tanner, for coming to see an old woman.'' Mrs. Johnson's small hand shook as she reached out and clasped his right arm. "Come in off the porch. It's too sticky out here. I made some lemonade for us.''

He wiped his boots on the mat in front of the door and followed the stooped woman inside. Although the rain had taken a break the last few hours, water still stood everywhere.

His Sunday had begun way too early, dark and grim. By now, the field resembled one huge mud pile, which eliminated an escape through work at the festival site.

Unwilling to sit around the big, gloomy house and dissect his argument with Cassie, which was the reason he hadn't slept well, he had finally remembered his promise to visit his dad's former math teacher. She had sounded thrilled over the prospect of a last-minute guest when he'd called.

The small house was dimly lit and cluttered, but clean. "Watch your step, Tanner. I find the lights hurt my eyes, so I just leave them off or turned way down. The kitchen has some natural light, though. It's just through here.''

Photos in various frames covered every flat surface. Books, stacked in neat piles next to the sofa and stuffed chair took the place of end tables.

"Have a seat, young man." She pointed to a chair at the small kitchen table. "I don't bake anymore, can't see well enough, but I get these at the bakery and they're almost as good as mine." She placed a plate of gingersnaps on the table in front of him, along with a glass of lemonade.

He took a cookie and a generous bite. "If yours were better, I'm sorry I missed them."

The old woman smiled. "Now I *know* you're Frankie's boy. He was quite the charmer. So, you've come to talk about the old days, about your dad."

"And my mom, Susan Daniels. She rarely talked about her family. All I know is that her dad had run off, and her mom couldn't handle the pressure of raising six kids alone and started drinking. And money was always tight. What happened to everyone?"

Mrs. Johnson shook her head and closed her eyes. "Such a sweet, smart, gentle girl. Such a hard life. They would've pulled her down with them if she hadn't left." The elderly woman opened her eyes, glistening with unshed tears. "Susan's mother was a damaged soul and died a few years back. All of her brothers were full of so much anger and bitterness. No one could reach them."

"Are any of them still around?"

"Dear me, no. Chief Randall ran them out of town at the first sign of trouble. I wouldn't be surprised to hear one or two are in prison somewhere. But what about your mother, Tanner? Was she happy?"

He gulped, caught off guard by the question. "I

think so. My parents loved each other very much. I just wish they'd had more time, together.''

Mrs. Johnson nodded. "We never know, do we? The whole town was in shock when we heard the news about your parents' accident. And so soon after losing your grandmother. It broke her heart to have her family torn apart so. Your grandfather eventually had a change of heart, but it was too late.''

Tanner could barely remember meeting his grandmother, since he was only five years old at the time, but nothing bad came to mind. His dad had explained that his grandmother loved him, but couldn't go against his grandfather's wishes—few people had the strength. She wasn't to blame.

He had learned of her death the same week his parents had died, so the news had hardly registered. ''No disrespect, Mrs. Johnson, but no one changes that much.''

"None taken. But you'd be surprised by what loss and a dose of humility can do, especially to a proud, stubborn man like your grandfather. He'd never lost at anything, until the day he found he couldn't control his son. Then he lost dear Elizabeth, your parents died, you were estranged. It humbled him.''

Tanner refused to feel pity for his grandfather. He'd brought any pain he might have experienced on himself. ''Too little, too late.''

"That's not for us to say, is it, dear? I do know that when your other grandmother was sick and couldn't pay her hospital bills, your grandfather stepped in. Even paid for her burial and plot out in the cemetery. He didn't want anyone to know, but there aren't many secrets in this town.''

Tanner hid his surprise. ''Just guilt money. He was

one of the reasons she never saw her daughter again.''

Mrs. Johnson reached across and put her wrinkled hand on his. ''If only life was so simple, Tanner. If only.''

Tanner squirmed in his seat. For some reason, he suddenly felt like one of Mrs. Johnson's students who'd been caught daydreaming in class. ''So, did you have some scrapbooks for me to look at?''

''Oh, yes. On the couch in the other room. Just bring in a few at a time.''

Tanner was overcome with the sense he'd missed something important, but what? They had only talked about the past.

He collected the books and wondered about the others stacked in piles up to three feet high around the room. How did she ever find anything specific? ''You could have your own library, Mrs. Johnson.'' He placed the scrapbooks on the table, and scooted his chair next to hers.

She chuckled softly. ''I know. Isn't it awful? But I find it comforts me, especially on my bad days when nothing seems to click in this old brain of mine. I had a boy ready to make bookcases for me, but he never showed up. I can't remember why, now. Doesn't matter, I suppose.''

''After we look at some pictures, maybe you could show me what you need and I could make them for you.''

''That would be wonderful, Tanner. You're an angel.''

Tanner didn't have the guts to contradict her. No angel would've treated Cassie so badly yesterday. One minute he'd been walking in the rain and kissing

Cassie senseless; he'd even confessed to his crazy thoughts when he first laid eyes on her.

When she had boldly asked him to stay in New Haven, a part of him yearned to hang around and experience a hayride and more with Cassie, the most curious, spontaneous, sensual woman he'd ever met.

Just the thought of staying, getting too settled, scared the hell out of him. So, he had lashed out with accusations about her and some deal she must have made with his grandfather.

Although she had never struck him as an opportunist, what else explained her determination to make him keep Fairfax House? She had looked tempted to slap him, and he didn't blame her.

At least he had a project to work on now. He would build a bookcase for a sweet old lady and hope the job would help keep his mind off how he alone was responsible for the hurt expression on Cassie's face before she'd walked away.

Monday morning, Cassie sat at her desk in her office and took an inventory of the room. She had just come from her meeting with a loan officer at the bank and was reminded again of all she could lose if her idea to turn Fairfax House into a boarding-house failed.

Wallpaper books of every size and color fought for room on the shelves that hugged walls painted a soft white with a touch of gray. Although a relatively small space, she had made it a priority for her office to have an enclosed area for kids to play while the harried parent, usually the mother, could take her time to look at samples of paint, paper, even window shades.

The door opened, and Georgie rushed in. "How did it go at the bank?"

"Okay, I guess."

Georgie took a seat across from Cassie. "Don't you think you're going a little overboard?"

"What do you mean?"

"What was your exact promise to Mr. Fairfax?"

"That I would do all I could to convince Tanner to keep Fairfax House and make it his home. We assumed that probably the only way that was going to happen was if he could finally forgive his grand-father. And now that Tanner and I had this huge fight, it's going to be even more difficult."

"I don't understand. Saturday afternoon you seemed convinced he'd stay. At the concert, you two didn't seem to know anyone else was around. What happened?"

Cassie wasn't about to admit she hadn't seen Georgie at the park. "He kissed me again and it made me forget my plan not to rush him. We ended up having an argument, and he said some pretty nasty things."

"That doesn't sound like Tanner. I mean, I don't know him that well, but, he doesn't come across like a jerk."

Cassie still reeled from his hurtful accusations. "He's not a jerk. The argument wasn't about me. He's still bitter about the past and lashing out. If I could just get him to read Mr. Frank's letter, it'd be a start. Tanner can't keep walking around with all that anger."

Georgie leaned forward in her chair. "I guess you're so intent on helping him because you went through the same thing when your dad died."

Cassie nodded. "Not exactly the same, but close enough to know Tanner will never find peace, never be happy until he can forgive. I had people to help me heal. Tanner's been alone since he was seventeen. I've got to help him, Georgie."

"I understand needing to try, but you're not a professional. You can only give it your best shot."

"No, I've got to do better than that. I never told anyone this, but I made a promise to my Dad just before he died and I couldn't keep it. I tried, but it was just too hard."

Surprise and sympathy flashed in Georgie's eyes. "I can't believe you've kept a secret all this time. What could a nine-year-old promise?"

"He wanted me to be more like my mom and Jill. Dad knew he wouldn't be around to be my buddy, do the tomboy things I liked to do. And, he knew my mom worried anyway that I'd never outgrow it. I lasted all of two days before I snapped and had to put on some ripped jeans and roll in the grass. I felt so guilty, but so good at the same time. I thought I'd do anything for my dad, but I just couldn't be a girlie-girl."

Georgie leaned forward and put her hand on Cassie's arm. "You still can't. And that's okay. Shoot, I'm surprised you lasted that long."

"I'm serious, Georgie."

"I know. But I truly believe not all promises should be kept. I'm sure your dad wanted what was best for you, but he was wrong. That's not your fault."

"But I want my word to mean something."

"Cassie, believe me, it does. Or you would never be the successful businessperson that you are."

"That's business. This is personal. Finally, I have the chance to prove my promise means something."

Georgie sighed and sat back in her chair. "I can see your mind is made up. I don't agree with your reasoning, but I back you a hundred percent whatever you decide to do."

"That's good to know, since I'm not giving up until the last possible moment. Besides, I've loved that house since I was a little girl. I couldn't bear to see it chopped up into an office building. I'll make it work. I have to."

Cassie couldn't lose the business she'd worked so hard to build, though. She was finally turning a profit and had just furnished her office.

The fairly new desk and the table and chairs for viewing materials were oak, with solid, simple lines. Filing cabinets held customer files, mailing lists, business contacts and any other paper related to her business.

"You'd be a great landlady. So, what are you going to do in the meantime?"

"I have no idea."

"You'd better come up with something. And quick. His time is almost up, isn't it?"

Cassie nodded. "Twenty days."

"That's not much time. And speaking of time, what's on the calendar for me today?"

Cassie gave Georgie her work orders for the day, collected the wallpaper for Fairfax House, then stopped by her apartment to change into bibs.

As she suspected, Tanner had already left for the festival site by the time she arrived at the house, and she was glad. Until she knew what to say to help change his mind about selling the estate, the less she saw of him the better.

She covered the kitchen floor with tarps before she set up her sawhorses and water tray. Grateful for the big job ahead, she measured for the first strip of wallpaper.

Excitement built inside Cassie as she hung each strip of paper. The white background sprinkled with small bouquets of spring flowers lightened up the room and opened up all sorts of possibilities for decorating.

She smiled as she imagined herself living at Fairfax House. Although she still hoped to change Tanner's mind, at least she had a backup plan to save the house. The white woodwork had added cheeriness. Plants would cover every ledge and soften the room. Even more important, love and laughter would fill the air. She could turn the house into a home.

"Cassie, the room looks wonderful."

Cassie glanced up to find her mother at the kitchen door. "Come on in, Mom."

She stepped inside and placed a gift sack on the table. "What has Tanner said about the changes?"

Cassie shrugged, then reached for another strip of wallpaper. "I haven't really seen him since Saturday night. And by the time he gets done out at Pete's, I'll be done here."

"I would've bet money that something was going on between you two the other night. Guess I was wrong. Do you think he's avoiding you?"

Cassie had no intention of reliving the heated argument between her and Tanner with her mother. Why depress them both? "I'm pretty sure it's because I pushed too hard about keeping Fairfax House, and now he's digging in his heels.''

She used a wide brush to force the wrinkles out from under the strip of wallpaper. Too bad she didn't have a magic tool that could erase the distrust Tanner felt about anything to do with his grandfather.

"Does this mean you're giving up on him?''

"No way. I'll figure something out.''

Diane chuckled. "If anyone can, you can. Meanwhile, on to Plan B?''

"Yep. I'm going to go ahead and bid on the house myself. He says he'll sell to the highest bidder, but I don't think he's that heartless. If it's between me and a law firm, he'll do the right thing.''

"I don't think it's a matter of being heartless. He's been hurt, Cassie. Men don't always know how to handle that. That's why I'm relieved to hear you two aren't involved. I don't want to see you get hurt.''

Cassie worried it was already too late. She cared way too much about wanting to erase the sadness in his eyes, and he seemed determined to hang onto a grudge, the very thing that caused him pain. "Well, Mom, there's nothing going on between us.'' At least, not anymore. "So, you don't have to worry.''

"Good. Anyway, I stopped by Donna's store for some candles and she asked me to tell you that your picture was ready. I thought I'd save you the trip and bring it over. I just grabbed a bag and paper on the way out.''

"Great. How does it look?''

Diane opened the sack and handed the gift to Cassie. "See for yourself.''

Cassie wiped her hands on a rag before she accepted the delicate silver frame. Tanner might look like his dad, but he had his mother's serious expression. Cassie couldn't even imagine how devastated he must've been to lose both parents so young. "This is great, Mom. We should give this to him together. When would be a good time?"

"Oh, no. It was your idea." Her mom kissed her on the cheek. "Gotta run. See you Thursday. I hope Tanner can come. I'll remind him. Bye now," she said, and drifted out the door.

Cassie started to warn her mother not to count on his company, but that would involve going into detail about their argument, so she kept silent. "Bye. And thanks."

She studied the picture of Tanner's parents, certain the answer to her problem rested in the past. If she could somehow get him to feel connected to his family's roots, she might still have a chance.

The dated clothes in the pictures of his parents reminded Cassie of the old things found in the storage room during her brief exploration of the upstairs. She had been moved to tears later while reading the love letters between Tanner's grandparents.

An idea began to form and she snapped her fingers. "I've got it." By Wednesday, she should be completely done with the kitchen. She'd come by once she knew he was home, have him inspect the job, and if satisfied, sign the work order.

She'd call a truce, pretend she accepted his decision to sell, and give him the picture of his parents. Then she would offer to help clean out the storage room. After all, the estate sale was only a couple of weeks away.

She just hoped and prayed she'd find something in the storage room that would help Tanner see beyond the pain of the past to the warmth and joy a sense of belonging could bring to him now.

Cassie felt a certain déjà vu standing at the front door of Fairfax House while she waited for Tanner to answer. Again, she had arrived with a gift and had ulterior motives for her visit. Had it really been less than two weeks ago?

"Cassie? What are you doing here? I mean, I was just about to walk over to your place."

She blinked, caught off guard. "You were?"

He nodded. "Can you come in for a minute?"

"Sure." She stepped inside and followed him to the kitchen. What could he possibly want to talk about? "So, what do you think of the kitchen? You can be honest, since you don't plan to stay."

"It looks fine. You did a great job, especially the cleanup. I tell my crews how important it is, but they hate doing it, so I have to ride them."

"That brings us to one reason why I came over. I need you to sign a work order." She handed him the paper and he signed. "Aren't you going to look over anything?"

"No. I trust you. And that's what I was coming over to your place to say. I owe you an apology for the other night. I took my anger at my grandfather out on you, and that's not fair. Even though I'll never understand why this house means so much to you, I don't think you made any deals with my grandfather."

"Apology accepted. And I would've told you right away about the private investigator, if you'd been the least bit reasonable about your grandfather."

"He made it pretty difficult. Truce?" Tanner held out his hand and she shook it.

She purposely ignored the heat of his touch. Relieved to have the argument behind them, she smiled. "Truce."

"You said the work order was one reason for stopping by. Was there another?"

"Oh, yes. I wanted to let you know that my real estate agent is getting the paperwork together and you'll receive my bid on the house Friday, as promised."

"So, you're really going through with it?"

"Of course. I just hope you won't hold it against me that we, well, sort of let our business relationship overlap into a personal one. If I'm wasting my time, tell me now."

"Nothing's changed. Money from the sale goes to charity, so I'm looking for the highest bid."

She forced herself not to wince. How silly of her to think a few mind-blowing kisses and a truce might affect his judgment. "Mine will be." At least greed wasn't motivating him to be a jerk. She held up the bag. "I have something for you."

"Look, I don't want—"

"It has nothing to do with the job or your grandfather or anything else. I just wanted to do this for you and my mom helped pull the idea together."

He studied the outstretched bag as if worried a snake nestled inside. "Go ahead, Tanner. It won't bite."

Tanner reluctantly accepted the gift. He disliked surprises, had experienced more bad ones than good. He tossed aside the bright-yellow paper and discovered something hard and silver. He pulled out a thin, scrolled picture frame—with photographs of his mom and dad.

Emotion tackled him, took the air from his lungs and any strength from his legs. He groped for the closest chair and sat, his gaze glued to the pictures. "This is incredible. Where did you find these?"

He traced the picture of his mother with his fingertips. Her expression revealed a lot of attitude instead of the tender smile he remembered. But then, her life had been pretty rough back then.

"I dug around some more in my mom's scrapbooks. You told me it didn't matter that you didn't have any pictures, but, no offense, I didn't believe you for a minute. I treasure the pictures I have of my father, even after all this time. Maybe more so. You hate to admit it, but after a while, you can't picture them in your mind, and you feel awful."

How often had he awakened in the night, in a panic because of a dream where he couldn't make out the details of his mother's face? The empathy reflected in Cassie's gaze touched his soul.

He forced his eyes wide-open to halt the threatening tears, a trick he learned a long time ago. "Thank you, Cassie. I don't know what else to say."

"That's all that's needed. You know, rule number—"

A nervous chuckle escaped his lips. "Rule number one in a small town."

"Right. I did have one other reason for dropping by, though. Mrs. Boone is swamped with helping the women's club get ready for the festival, and she wanted me to ask if you'd consider donating some of your family memorabilia to the Historical Society.

I'd be glad to help you go through the stuff. You'll have to clean out the storage closet upstairs anyway, if you're going to have an estate sale.''

He'd never admit it, but he dreaded the idea of doing the huge job himself. ''How did you know about the...? Never mind. Sure, that would be great. I was going to start by sorting the obvious junk first. You could go through papers and pictures, since you'd know more what might be valuable. When would be a good time?''

''Now is good.''

He hesitated, suspicious of her eagerness to help, but not sure why. Heck, she'd just given him an amazing gift, proof she was generous. He had no reason to question her motives. Besides, work would help level off his emotions. ''Great. Let's go.''

She followed him upstairs and immediately zeroed in on the desk. While she rifled through the drawers, he picked a corner of the room and started two piles, one for obvious junk, the other for questionable items that he'd ask Cassie about later.

Why did people hang on to so much useless stuff? he wondered, as he tossed a chewed-up ball into the junk pile.

''Tanner, can you help me? The lid is stuck.''

He turned around to find Cassie kneeling next to an old trunk. ''Sure.'' With a fist, he pounded at the seam of the lid and base, but it refused to budge.

After several tries, the lid finally gave and out tumbled dresses and slips made of light-blue and lilac silk. A black tuxedo jacket and pants followed, along with a top hat and gloves.

''What a find!'' Cassie cheered as she held up each dress for inspection. ''I think I remember seeing

a picture of your grandmother in this purple dress.''
Cassie wiggled into the silky creation. "Can't you
just imagine the glamour of the good old days? The
high teas and balls?" She handed Tanner the jacket.
"Here, try this on."

Her enthusiasm contagious, Tanner grinned and
shrugged into the jacket. "Why not? We deserve a
break. How about some music? Would you believe
the Victrola still works? It just needed a little cleaning up." He walked over to a box next to the antique.
"I found these records the other day when I started
going through stuff." He grabbed the top 78 titled
"Well, Get It!" by Tommy Dorsey, put it on the
turntable, and rotated the crank on the Victrola several times. With a flip of a lever, the turntable began
to spin and he moved the arm with the needle over
onto the outer rim of the record.

A jazzy instrumental, albeit a little fuzzy sounding,
filled the room. "Shall we dance?" He held out his
hand.

Cassie's expression changed from surprise to
delight. The hundred-watt smile she sent his way was
more than enough reward for his spontaneous gesture. If he wasn't careful, it could become a habit.

She curtsied and placed her small hand in his. The
perfect song for a fast waltz, he led her across the
narrow room, sidestepping the piles of trash and treasure.

A scratching sound signaled the end of the song.
"One more song, Tanner. Please?"

She glanced up at him with those sparkling green
eyes and there was no way he could say no—even
if he wanted to. "Sure. I'll just turn this one over."

He hurried to the Victrola, repeated the process in

reverse, and returned to Cassie, ready for another rousing number.

Instead, Frank Sinatra sang "I'll Be Seeing You," a slow, romantic ballad that left Tanner's feet glued to the floor. The words to the song, the longing in Sinatra's voice made Tanner realize how much he'd miss Cassie when he was gone.

Awareness charged every particle of air in the room. The smiles stopped.

He couldn't tear his gaze away from her beautiful face, any more than he could resist the chance to hold Cassie close one more time before he left. Pulling her closer, her hardened nipples pressed against his chest as she swayed against him. She drove him crazy with need, but that was only part of the attraction.

She continually did or said something that made him feel connected to her in a way he'd never before experienced. The way she had sensed how much he'd wanted a picture of his mom, then followed through, had touched his soul. The way she held him eased the restlessness in his heart.

He had to have her.

Chapter Nine

Cassie gave no thought to resisting as Tanner pulled her against him. His hands, so strong and warm, splayed against her back. She absorbed the wonderful sensation of his touch, inhaled the scent that belonged only to Tanner.

Between the old-fashioned silk dress and Sinatra's rich voice singing "I'll be seeing you, in all the old familiar places...." Cassie felt as if she'd been transported back in time. A time where nothing stood in the way of her and Tanner being together.

His hands caressed her back with excruciating gentleness, as if she might break if he held her too tight. But she didn't want him afraid of anything. She wasn't fragile.

She wrapped her arms around his neck and molded her body against his. She wanted more. So much more. With a groan, his mouth hungrily sought hers. His hands cupped her bottom, pressing her against his hardness, and she thrilled at the knowledge she was responsible for his arousal.

The intense chemistry, their similar professions, his restless heart and her settled one...they combined for a perfect fit. She closed her eyes and dared to dream as she pictured the two of them, together at Fairfax House, raising a family and surrounded by love.

Caught up in the music of days long past, she could no longer deny she had lost her heart to Tanner, so tough-minded yet tender.

She knew him better than he knew himself. He'd realize before it was too late that they were meant for each other.

The needle scratched against the rim of the vinyl record. Tanner's hands stilled. He tore his mouth away from hers, his breathing ragged, his face white.

He tried to step back, out of her embrace, but she held tight. "Not again, Tanner. Don't pull away again."

"I have to. I don't want to hurt you."

"Then don't. We're a lot alike, Tanner. We've both lost loved ones, we both had to become adaptable and self-reliant because of it. But I was lucky. I didn't have to go through it by myself. If only you'd give the town a chance, me a chance, you'd realize you don't have to be alone."

"Nothing has changed, Cassie. In two weeks I leave town. We both know a fling is not what you want, and it's certainly not what you deserve."

Cassie flinched, his words a fist to her heart. She stepped out of his arms and held her chin high. "You're right. I do deserve better, but then, so do you. It's a shame you can't see that. I feel sorry for you, Tanner. You push away the people who care about you. You'll never find happiness that way."

She pulled the dress over her head and gently laid it across the trunk. "Goodbye, Tanner."

"Cassie, hon, I know baking bread isn't your favorite thing to do, but you're worse than usual tonight," Diane chided and put a hand on Cassie's arm. "You need a teaspoon of baking powder, not baking soda. Want to talk about what's bothering you?"

Cassie usually found comfort in her mom's cozy kitchen, with the mouthwatering smells and easy smiles. But tonight, all she could think about was how she and Tanner had almost made love, and how her goodbye to Tanner had sounded so final. "I'm not in the mood to talk, Mom."

She didn't feel like explaining how her heart ached for Tanner, for his sake, though, not hers, or so she told herself. She refused to waste any more of her emotions on someone who looked at life and love so differently because it would only lead to heartache. End of subject.

"Okay. But I'm here if you need me. I'm sorry Tanner couldn't make it tonight. He seemed to enjoy himself last time."

"He did, or he wouldn't have sent you the cookie presses, right?"

Diane smiled. "So much like his dad. Frankie never did the standard flowers or candy, but always made his gifts so personal. One time, Frankie gave me a pin in the shape of a kitten for my birthday because I had rescued a stray and adopted it."

Cassie didn't care if Tanner was a romantic like

his dad. She should never have allowed herself to daydream. No more. Time to return to her usual, practical self. "Yeah, well, too bad Tanner doesn't feel anything personal toward his family estate. I just don't get it. I've tried everything to help him understand the importance of roots, to make him feel like he belongs here in New Haven and at Fairfax House. He's letting his bitterness toward his grandfather cloud his judgement."

"He just needs time, Cassie."

"But I only have a little more than two weeks left. If I don't figure out a way to get Tanner to see his grandfather for the man he became, not the man he once was, Tanner will sell and go back to Texas. I promised Mr. Frank I wouldn't let that happen."

"No, you promised to try. And I really don't think Frank expected you to risk the very business he sold you, to save the house. I mean, if Fairfax House becomes an office building, it will be a shame, but not the end of the world. If you can't make a go of the boardinghouse idea, you could lose both the house *and* your business. That wouldn't be just a shame, that would be devastating. Are you sure you've thought this through?"

"Mom, there's more." Cassie explained the promise she had made to her father and then failed to keep. "I let him down. I let you down."

Her mother hugged her tight, then held herself back in order to look her daughter in the eyes, although the tears must have gotten in the way some. "Now you listen to me, Cassie Leighton," she said sternly, her voice shaking with emotion. "You didn't let either of us down. Your dad meant well, but he was wrong to ask you to change. You are perfect just the way you are. I'm proud of you and he would be, too. The truth is, not all promises should be kept."

Now Cassie had trouble seeing through her own tears. "I want my word to mean something. This is my chance to prove to Mr. Frank, to Dad, to myself, that it does."

"There's nothing I can say to convince you otherwise?"

"I'm afraid not." She grabbed a napkin from the table and dried her eyes while her mom did the same. "So, have you heard from Jill lately?"

"Finally." Her mom sighed. "I'm so worried about her living on her own in the city. I'll bet she's not eating. She sounded so distant...."

Cassie half listened to her mother's long list of worries, thankful to have the spotlight on someone else.

The next morning, Tanner arrived at the festival site hours before anyone else. Although he had no reason to hurry from the house to avoid Cassie—her work was done—sleep had eluded him and he couldn't stand one more minute in the huge, empty house.

What had he been thinking the other night? If Cassie could attach so much importance to a house and a town, who knew what she might attach to making love?

Because he cared, he wasn't about to take that chance; he refused to take advantage of her trusting nature. But doing the right thing was greatly overrated. Even though he felt noble for dredging up the willpower to halt making love to Cassie, he was miserable.

He blamed his grandfather. If he hadn't attached the blasted live-in clause to the inheritance, Tanner would never have come to New Haven, never met Cassie.

But then he would've never been on the receiving end of her killer smile and generous nature, would've never realized how much he missed spontaneity in his life.

Damn. Since when couldn't he depend on summoning anger toward his grandfather?

"You're out here early, Tanner."

Tanner looked up to find Pete next to him, his injured foot covered in a soft cast. "Yeah, well, there's a lot to do. How's the ankle coming along?"

"Real good. I can't thank you enough for taking over here."

"It's the least I could do. I've never forgotten that first time we met, how you took the time to talk to me."

"I've always liked to talk. Glad if I helped some."

"You did, except I think all I got out of what you said was that you must've been blind if you could compare a butterfly to an old, wrinkled man like my grandfather."

Pete chuckled. "I think I also said something about, hopefully some day, your grandfather would get smart and learn how to let go. He did, you know."

Tanner shook his head. "Not you, too. I swear, between you, other people in this town and Cassie, you'd think the man died a saint."

"Not a saint, Tanner, just repentant. He started changing after your parents died, and then even more toward the end."

"So, all should be forgiven—" Tanner snapped his fingers "—just like that?"

"Read the letter Frank wrote to you. At least your grandfather found it hard to let go out of love, and don't think for a minute he didn't love you or your dad. Maybe it's time to let go of all that anger. Just something to think about."

Pete limped away and Tanner stared at his retreating back.

Just what he didn't need, another advocate for his grandfather. Fortunately, his "sentence" at Fairfax House was almost up. Fifteen days and counting.

An image of Cassie sprung into his mind, her sad expression when she had said goodbye. Suddenly, the little over two weeks he had left didn't seem as long as before.

Wednesday evening, Cassie fetched her mail and trudged up the narrow steps to her apartment, bone weary, drained in spirit, and numb at heart.

Unfortunately, not even long workdays could drown out the countdown in her mind of the days left before the live-in clause expired on Fairfax House. Only four more days before Tanner left town and took her heart with him.

She listlessly flipped through her mail then froze at the sight of familiar, chicken-scratch handwriting. Impossible. The letter couldn't be from Mr. Frank.

Hands shaking, Cassie opened the envelope and gingerly pulled out the letter.

My Dearest Cassie,
I gave this letter to Mr. Samuels, with instructions to mail it on the twenty-fifth day of my

estate's live-in clause. By now you've surely met my grandson, Tanner. I told you that my wish was for him to forgive me and make Fairfax House his home. Selfish of me, I know. But I must confess I had hopes of giving my grandson not only a house, but a chance at real love, the kind of love his parents had shared. My fondest wish is that the two of you discover you are perfect for one another. My restless grandson deserves a real home, deserves love, and who better for him than you, dear, with your heart as big as Texas?

If my clumsy attempt at matchmaking is unsuccessful, please don't think too harshly of me. The house is secondary. I only wanted the best for the two people I care most about.

Affectionately,
Frank Fairfax II

Tears plopped onto the page and Cassie quickly jerked the letter out of the way. She wiped the tears from her face with her fingers, stunned to discover she'd been duped. Not once had she suspected the old coot of having ulterior motives for involving her in his campaign to save his family estate.

Too bad his matchmaking plans had gone up in smoke.

Mr. Frank had been manipulative until the day he died, as Tanner had claimed, but not for the reasons imagined. Finally, she had proof of Mr. Frank's change of heart. She would read the letter out loud to Tanner if she had to.

Although the memory of Tanner's rejection still

stung, she refused to let her pride get in the way of keeping a promise.

Tanner took another drink of beer and grimaced. Just four more days, he thought, as he sat at the kitchen table with the three contracts for the house in front of him. He had assumed that a couple of beers would help set the mood to celebrate that his "sentence" at Fairfax House was almost over. But the beer tasted flat, and it had nothing to do with an expiration date.

He had the blues because he missed Cassie, missed her laugh and her flair for wearing hats. Most of all, he missed the way she made him feel whole when he held her.

He hadn't expected Cassie to come running to him after he had rejected her, but he had assumed he would've at least seen her around town.

She was either extremely busy, or avoiding him, maybe both. And why shouldn't she? He had only thrown away probably the best thing that had ever happened to him. But he couldn't change now and be joined at the hip with someone, and that remained a fact. It was time to move on.

He stared at the contracts. He wouldn't even consider the one ridiculously low bid. Although reasonable, Cassie's offer ran several thousand short.

Tanner signed the law firm's contract, a purely logical decision that would benefit a charity he really believed in.

That Fairfax House should become an office building only made the justice sweeter, almost poetic.

He waited for a sense of peace to settle over him, but his spirits remained as flat as the beer. Might as well get started packing. He left the kitchen and headed for the stairs.

Several hard knocks on the kitchen door made him pause. "What now?" he mumbled, and begrudgingly turned around and made his way back to the kitchen.

The sight of Cassie on the other side of the screen door made him stop midstride. She wore a strained smile along with a denim hat, T-shirt and his favorite form-fitting jeans.

He had missed her more than he cared to admit.

What would've dragged her to Fairfax House, to him, after she had clearly said goodbye?

She seemed pale. Maybe it was just the lighting.

"I just need a minute, Tanner."

"Cassie, what is it?" He opened the door and she stepped inside. The lighting hadn't been the problem at all. She was wearing heavy makeup that had managed to cover all but a hint of dark circles beneath her eyes.

Every nerve ending screamed for him to touch her, comfort her. But what would he say? Nothing had changed.

"I got this in the mail today," she said. "It's a postdated letter from your grandfather."

Tanner frowned. Here we go again. The man could manipulate from the grave.

"I know what you're thinking, Tanner, but you're wrong. Here, read it for yourself." She held out the envelope.

He shook his head and crossed his arms across his chest.

"Okay. Then, I will." She removed the letter and tossed the envelope on the table. "What's this?" She peered at the papers he had left out. Her hand shook as she picked up the signed contract and read. "How could you?" Tears welled up in her eyes.

Tanner knew, at that moment, he'd been crazy to deny how much Cassie meant to him. "Please don't take it personally, Cassie. This is strictly business. I had already decided to donate the money from the sale of the house to a charity. It's an organization that helped me after my parents died. A lot of good will come from this."

"Who are you kidding? The main reason you're doing this is to get back at your grandfather."

"My grandfather's wishes mean nothing to me. I don't care about Fairfax House, I care about you."

"You do?"

He put his hands on her shoulders and met her gaze. "When I first got here, I was counting the days until I could leave. Now, I'm having trouble remembering why I have to go."

"Oh, Tanner." She threw her arms around his neck and kissed him with a passion that almost buckled his legs. Suddenly, she grew stiff and tore her mouth away. Her once joyful expression turned serious. "Wait a minute. You care for me, but you're still leaving? Why can't you stay, stay and live at Fairfax House?"

"I'd never get used to an entire town knowing my business. And if I keep the house it will mean my grandfather has won. Come to Texas with me. We can build our own future, without any ties to the past."

Cassie somehow found the strength to step out of Tanner's embrace, one of the hardest things she'd ever made herself do. She was thrilled to hear Tanner cared for her, knew what it had cost him to admit his feelings and ask her to go away with him, but she had yet to hear that he loved her.

She refused to turn her life upside down on something that could turn out to be a whim. "What kind of future can we have until you can accept the past, accept your grandfather for the real person he was, both good and bad, and forgive? If you can't do that, the future will be empty."

"But, Cassie—"

"We need to learn from the mistakes of others and not waste precious time," she pushed on. "Stay. Give what we have between us a fighting chance. We can be full partners, Tanner. Our careers mesh perfectly. The whole town has accepted you as one of their own. We *both* belong here. Can't you see that?"

"No. You're asking too much. I'd suffocate with all that togetherness. I've been on my own too long."

"I do care about you, Tanner, but I could never just abandon my business, or leave my friends and family. And even if I could, I'm not foolish enough to turn away from all that's important to me for a man who only wants to give me a piece of himself. It's all or nothing with me, Tanner." Cassie tossed the contract and Mr. Frank's letter onto the table, choked back the tears and left Fairfax House for the last time.

Her worst fears had come true—she had lost the battle to save Fairfax House and lost her heart to the wrong man.

"Cassie! Are you in there? It's Georgie. Open the door."

Cassie groaned, irritated over being pulled out of

a deep sleep. She forced her eyes open and glanced at the alarm clock. Ten! No way. She never over-slept. But then again, she'd never had her heart so trampled on before, either. "I'm coming. Hold your horses."

Cassie grabbed her robe and left to open the door.

"Oh, my gosh. You look terrible. Do you have a fever?" Georgie put her hand on Cassie's forehead. "No fever. Does your stomach hurt?"

Tears filled Cassie's eyes at the concern in Georgie's voice. "You're adorable when you slip into mom mode."

Georgie grimaced. "I doubt my last date thought so when I told him to eat his vegetables."

Cassie attempted a smile and failed.

"Here. This was attached to your door."

Cassie opened the envelope and pulled out a note and folded piece of paper. "You were right, Cassie," she read aloud. "I made my decision for the wrong reason. You obviously love this house and I want you to have it. The lawyer can contact me in Tyler if he needs to. I never meant to hurt you and hope someday you can forgive me. Tanner."

She quickly unfolded the paper and was stunned to find her contract, now signed. Fairfax House would be hers. She waited for relief or excitement to wash over her, but instead she felt drained, empty.

"Mr. Frank would be so proud of you, Cassie. You saved Fairfax House from being ripped apart and made into offices. We need to celebrate."

Cassie was miserable. She couldn't fool herself any longer. She loved Tanner. And even if he loved her, and was just too afraid to admit it, he was leaving. "Yeah, that's good news."

Georgie took Cassie by the arm and led her to the couch in the small family room. "Wait a minute. You're not beating yourself up because you think you failed to keep your promise, are you? Because, I know you did everything possible."

Cassie leaned into Georgie's shoulder and the tears fell freely. After she was finally cried out, she pulled a tissue from her robe pocket and blew her nose. "I've been such a fool, Georgie."

"Let me guess. This isn't about the house at all or the promise. It's about you and Tanner."

Cassie nodded. "I tried not to fall in love with him. I knew the risks, but I convinced myself that in the end he wouldn't be able to just walk away, that his feelings for me were too strong."

"I'm guilty of having done the same thing, Cas. I thought that when Emily was born, Ray would realize what really mattered and choose his family over the gambling. But, he either couldn't or wouldn't."

"Anyone who could walk away from you and Emily is a jerk. He's lucky you only divorced him after he cleaned out your savings. He should've ended up in jail."

Georgie nodded. "I'm just glad that part of my life is over. Emily is with me and is my whole world. But we're done talking about me. Tanner could still change his mind. There are still a few days left."

Cassie shook her head. "He won't. He admitted he cares for me and asked me to go back to Texas with him. No matter how much I love him, I can't do it."

"Of course you can't. Unless, well, maybe this is his way of testing to see how much you love him."

Cassie thought of the letters she'd read from Mr.

Frank to his wife while thousands of miles away at war. Neither time nor distance had faded their love for one another. But that certainly didn't hold true for everyone.

"Maybe he wants to know which means more to you," Georgie continued. "The house and your business, both with ties to his grandfather, or him?"

"It isn't that simple. Even if I could make myself leave New Haven, until he can let go of the hate he feels for his grandfather, he'll never be happy, and that's bound to affect us. And just as important, he's totally against the idea of working together, and you know how I feel about that."

Georgie nodded. "But, how do you know if it would even work out? You'd be spending nearly every moment of every day together. You like your independence, running your own business. Do you really want to share, let someone else have a say in what you do and how you do it?"

"I at least want the chance to try. I want someone willing to give it a try."

"You're not leaving any room here for compromise, Cas."

"No one knows how long they'll have together. Think of how much time my parents missed out on because my dad worked so much. And look what happened to Jill. I don't want to waste time apart chasing different dreams."

"Jill had other problems in her marriage. You need to figure out what *you* need to be happy. If it's complete togetherness, then you shouldn't settle for less. At least Tanner was honest about it and didn't string you along. Believe me, that's worse."

Cassie hugged Georgie, who knew first-hand the

pain caused by empty promises. "I know, Georgie. But it still hurts."

Dusk had settled, and the walls seemed to close in on Tanner. Yesterday he had helped with the finishing touches at the festival site, so he had no reason to return. The Thunderbird had been picked up a couple of days ago, so he couldn't even tinker with the car.

Tanner intended to leave early the next morning before the parade, hoping to avoid goodbyes from the people who had so willingly welcomed him to their town, into their lives.

One more night at Fairfax House and then back to his old life. Why wasn't he excited or at least relieved at the prospect?

He already knew the answer to the question. Throughout the mansion, reminders of Cassie blindsided him. When he climbed the stairs, he'd remember her slow ascent after years of waiting to explore. She brought out a spontaneity in him that he had thought long gone.

Every time he entered the kitchen, he'd smell the vanilla left in a pan on the stove and recall the tears in Cassie's eyes as she explained the meaning behind the spice.

At the table, he'd recall the way Cassie had savored the cinnamon roll and brought his senses alive. Even the ridiculous plant on the windowsill, many of its leaves now yellow, served as a constant reminder of her impact on his life. He felt guilty, even though he shouldn't. He never wanted the blasted plant in the first place.

He gave the ivy some water.

Every place and thing sparked memories too vivid to forget, made him want to ignore why he should leave town and instead count the reasons why he should stay.

Whenever he passed by the door to the closet under the staircase, the memory of their first kiss would send him reeling. A visit to the storage room proved even more painful as he recalled how they had danced, touched and almost made love.

Enough.

What was done was done. She had asked for more than he had to give. Time to get back to Texas and the life he'd known before Cassie.

He had already gone through each room upstairs and gathered his stuff into his dufflebag. That just left the downstairs to inspect.

After a quick tour through the front rooms, he ended up in the kitchen, the biggest reminder of Cassie. She had left her imprint on everything, from the clean white woodwork to the cheery wallpaper. Because of her, the room had become more welcoming and warm.

The kitchen table remained littered with the papers and envelopes from Cassie's last visit just two nights ago. He recalled how quickly the color had drained from her face once she had seen the law firm's contract, signed. Was she happy now? Lord, he hoped so.

But what could his grandfather have written to make Cassie think it would make a difference? Curiosity got the better of him. He picked up his grandfather's letter and strained to read the scratchy, sprawling handwriting.

Tanner shook his head. Impossible. The man who

had made his family's life a living hell could not have written such a letter. *This* person claimed his grandson's happiness was more important than the family estate. The man who Tanner swore had ice water in his veins had turned into Cupid. Unbelievable.

Stunned by the emotional letter from a man Tanner had thought incapable of feeling, he rummaged through his dufflebag for the other letter from his grandfather and ripped open the envelope.

Tanner wasn't sure why he'd kept the letter, let alone brought it with him, except for the off chance the lawyer might require any and all correspondence to settle the estate.

Or had that been the only reason? Maybe some long-buried need to reconcile with the past had kept him from throwing it away like he had the others.

Tears pooled in Tanner's eyes as he read again about his grandfather's regrets over giving his wife everything but what she had truly wanted, a truce with their son so that they could be a family again.

Finally, Tanner could allow himself to mourn the loss of his grandmother who had never stopped loving him or given up hope for a reconciliation.

Tanner continued to read how years ago, his grandfather had claimed to want the best for Tanner, that he wanted to give him all the advantages money and the family name could bring, which meant the boy needed to live at Fairfax House. What he realized later on, was that he'd also hoped to bring Tanner's father to his knees and admit he'd been wrong to turn his back on his family. A power play which had caused Tanner's family to pull together even more and distance themselves further from the person who threatened their happiness.

Too much pride, selfishness and stubbornness had ruined any chance of a truce. Eventually, his grandfather had grown to regret trying to break up Tanner's family, but the damage had been done. He only hoped that someday he'd be forgiven.

Since the moment he had decided to claim his inheritance, Tanner believed he was doing so to attain justice in his parents' name. But now he realized he had sought revenge for himself. What had ever made him think his parents would have approved? Despite her harsh childhood, he'd never heard his mom blame anyone. His dad had risked rejection again and attempted a reconciliation with his father after five years of silence.

As a grown man, Tanner should have known to ignore the promise he'd made at his parents' graves as a scared seventeen-year-old boy. Deep down, he had considered himself a coward for being afraid to face his grandfather and make him pay, when all along, maybe he'd pushed the vow aside because he had known in his gut that revenge, thinly masked as justice, was wrong.

Because of his own pride and stubbornness, Tanner had missed the chance to reunite with the one family member left.

Tanner hung his head in shame. Tears flowed from his eyes, cleansing him of years of pent-up bitterness and pain. But how could he ever forgive himself for letting hate consume him? For not being as brave as his father and reaching out to someone who had hurt him?

Tanner wiped his face with his shirttail. The painful realization hit that he was more like his grandfather than he cared to admit.

That Cassie had found something to love in the old man amazed Tanner. That she claimed to have feelings for *him*, despite his many faults, amazed him even more.

He'd been too selfish to even consider her desire for full partnership with the person she loved. So stubborn and hell-bent on revenge, he had hurt her by rejecting her bid on the house; so proud, he refused to admit he needed her. He had come to believe that needing someone reflected a weakness, and wasn't worth the risk since they always left you one way or another.

He didn't want to die a lonely man with regrets, always wondering if he should've taken a chance on love. With Cassie's help, he might even learn to forgive himself for throwing away the chance to mend fences with his grandfather before he died.

Tanner was still unsure about working together, but he'd give it a shot on a trial basis, if she would still have him.

Twelve hours and counting. Not much time to come up with a way to get and keep Cassie's attention long enough to beg for forgiveness and another chance.

He had helped quite a few people during his stay in New Haven. Maybe it was *his* turn to ask a few favors of his own.

Chapter Ten

Cassie paced the weathered floor of the tiny alcove of her apartment, alternately glancing across the street at Fairfax House and down at the contract that assured her ownership of the property.

Today was the last day of Tanner's live-in requirement. His truck was nowhere in sight. Had he already gone? She had to do something, but what?

Muffled music from marching bands miles away sprinkled the air. The sun was out with no sign of rain, a great day to open the Founder's Day festival.

Normally, she'd be as excited as a child about the parade that would slowly make its way down Main Street until it passed by in front of her apartment. But pleasure remained the last thing on her mind, and not even the fact that the For Sale sign had disappeared from the front lawn of Fairfax House could lighten her spirits.

She had originally thought that convincing Tanner to stay and saving the house were her only goals. But she had fallen in love with Tanner, and now all she could think about was *if only*. If only he had been able to forgive his grandfather and make peace with the past, they could've had a future together.

The other things, living in Fairfax House, working together, those would be nice, but not necessary for her happiness. But she had insisted on all or nothing, and look at what she'd ended up with: a house that meant nothing to her without Tanner.

She'd been a fool to think a partnership of any kind could survive without compromise.

The conversation with her mother still echoed in Cassie's mind. Men don't always know how to handle pain. She knew firsthand there wasn't a time limit on grief. Healing of any kind proceeded at its own pace.

Until now, she hadn't realized how unfair she'd been to ask Tanner to trust in their love, when *she* was the one determined to hedge her bets by insisting on a complete partner, what she thought would guarantee permanence.

Well, not anymore. The past few days had given her a glimpse of her life without him. If she truly loved Tanner, she'd accept him for the man he was, a man who needed lots of space for his restless heart to feel at home.

She'd be patient until Tanner could let go of the bitterness toward his grandfather. Mr. Frank had taken years to realize his mistakes, yet Cassie had stood by him. Why should she do less for Tanner?

The faded letters between Tanner's grandparents proved love could survive any obstacle; both of their parents had chosen the right partners as well. She knew in her heart that she and Tanner were also meant to be together.

She just needed a chance to convince him that with a little give and take, their love would not only grow but endure.

Unable to remain in her apartment another minute, she decided to first make sure Fairfax House was empty, and if it was, she'd then find Mr. Samuels, even if it meant dragging him out of the parade, and ask for Tanner's address in Texas. She'd go after him, and he would hear what she had to say, whether he wanted to or not.

She hurried downstairs and out the door, across the porch, and onto the sidewalk pointed toward Fairfax House. The sudden blast of a horn slowed her steps. She looked over her right shoulder to find the lead car of the parade, Mr. Frank's Thunderbird, in the distance. Everyone in the convertible waved frantically. But why? She wasn't in any danger so far away.

The car drew closer. No mistake, the man in the front passenger seat was Mr. Samuels. Good. She wouldn't have to go looking for him. Three boys scrunched in the back.

The driver continued to wave as the wind flicked at his coal-black hair. Those broad shoulders and muscled, tanned arms could only belong to one person—Tanner!

Her heart beat faster and faster. She couldn't believe Tanner was still in town, let alone leading the parade. Was it a sign he'd changed his mind about leaving?

Tanner had to make a conscious effort to keep the Thunderbird at the painfully slow parade speed, especially after he'd observed Cassie hesitate at the curb across from Fairfax House.

"This is a good omen, young man," the lawyer said and patted him on the shoulder. "What are the odds of Cassie appearing just as we arrive? It's fate, I tell you."

"Yeah, it's gotta mean something good," Cory chimed in.

Allen grinned and bobbed his head up and down.

"You have the cool car. How can you lose?" Ben dead-panned.

Tanner chuckled, pleased that Ben now felt comfortable enough to joke around. He was one of the reasons that made the decision to stay a little easier, but certainly not the most important.

Hours earlier, when he had shared his plan with Mr. Samuels, the mayor and anyone else within earshot, the warm reception of the townspeople had reaffirmed his decision to stay. Their acceptance might have been solely based on his last name at the beginning, but now they knew and accepted him for who he was, as a person.

Then again, only one person's opinion really mattered. "I hope you're right."

Cassie remained as still as a statue at the curb. Was she just in shock to find him leading the parade? Or still so mad at him that she refused to show any emotion at all? Either way, he'd have his say.

Tanner stopped the convertible, and the parade, in front of Fairfax House, then hurried out of the car toward Cassie.

His heart pounded like a jackhammer in his ears and drowned out the noise of the bands and the crowd. He reached for Cassie, worried he'd be rejected, since he'd already turned her away, but even more afraid of giving up on his only chance of happiness.

Cassie threw her arms around his neck and he lifted her off the ground, holding her tight against him, her tears warm on his neck. "I read the letters, Cassie. I'm sorry for being such a fool." Her tears fell even harder. "You were right not to accept my halfhearted offer to leave New Haven. I promise I won't hold anything back. I love you, want to marry you and fill Fairfax House with kids and grandkids. I'll even give working together a shot. On a trial basis."

He cupped her tearstained face with his hands and looked into her eyes. "Please tell me that I'm not too late."

"These are tears of happiness, Tanner," she said, her voice unsteady. "I was on my way to Fairfax House to tell you that I love you and to make a similar offer. I was afraid that what we had between us wasn't strong enough, but now I'm sure it is. I still think it would be fun to work together, but if it doesn't work out, it's no big deal. What really matters is that we're together."

Tanner nodded. "I'm going to need your help on this forgiveness thing, Cassie. You were right about having regrets. When I think of how I threw away the chance to know my grandfather, the only family I had left…"

"You've taken the first step. The rest will come. I promise I'll be here for you." She placed her hand on his cheek. "Always."

He moved her hand to his mouth, kissed the palm, then held it against his heart. "I can't believe just thirty days ago I cursed my grandfather for manipulating me into coming here, and now I just wish there was some way to thank him.''

She wiped away her tears with her other hand and smiled. ''Being together and making Fairfax House our home will be enough thanks. I'll bet he's smiling right now.''

''So, you don't think he'd mind if we carve some initials of our own in a certain closet under a staircase?''

''He'd love it!'' Cassie tilted her head to one side and grinned. ''You know, I'll bet he wouldn't mind a few great-grandchildren to go along with those initials.''

Tanner looked down at the woman who had so profoundly changed his life in just a month's time. Finally, he was right where he belonged. ''I'm counting the days.''

He pulled Cassie into his arms and poured his heart and soul, his promise to love her forever, into his kiss.

The whole town cheered, and car horns blasted, and drums, and tubas and trumpets played on. But the craziness barely registered. He was lost in Cassie's kisses, which promised a future full of warmth, light, laughter, and above all, love.

Epilogue

Fourteen months later

Tanner squinted against the October sun as he hurried up the steps of Fairfax House. The hum of overlapping conversations sailed on a breeze from the front rooms onto the porch through the opened windows.

He opened the heavy front door to a throng of people and the ever present scent of vanilla. Light poured into the front rooms, now free of dark, heavy drapes. Elegant furniture temporarily hugged the walls so that people had more room to gather and mingle.

"Great party, young Fairfax."

"Mommy, where's the open house? I wanna see a open house."

"Emily, sweetheart, I already explained what that really means."

"Did you see that incredible spoon collection? Must be worth a pretty penny."

Tanner smiled at the mention of the spoons as he made a path through the well-wishers toward Cassie. Sure, the collection was impressive, but the true value lay in what it represented—the importance of family and learning from mistakes.

Although his grandfather had been the one responsible for tearing the family apart, he'd also gone to great lengths to give his grandson what he'd been cheated out of—a sense of where he belonged, his roots.

Together, he and Cassie would ensure that his grandfather's memory would live on not only in the community, but in his family.

Tanner finally reached Cassie, surrounded by neighbors and friends eager for a peak at four-month-old Susan Diane Fairfax, named after her grandmothers, and called Susie for short.

Cassie glanced up, as if sensing his return. Dark-green eyes sparkled and her smile still knocked the breath out of him. "Sorry it took so long, hon." He placed his daughter's favorite rattle in her tiny right hand, then draped his arm around Cassie, careful not to tip her favorite floppy denim hat.

Contentment, a sensation he'd only rediscovered during the past year, settled over him.

His daughter cooed and his gaze returned to the newborn miracle. She had the dark Fairfax hair and eyes, but her mom's pert nose. With his free hand, he gently brushed her soft cheek, only to have her grip one of his fingers with her other hand.

He chuckled. In reality, *she* had *him* wrapped around her delicate finger and he didn't mind one bit. Did every Dad feel so blessed, honored, protective? He swallowed the lump of emotion in his throat.

"I saw Mr. Samuels talking to you earlier," Cassie said. "Anything important?"

"His wife saw how you fixed up the old storage area into a play room, and wants you to fix up their attic for her grandkids. He's going to talk to you later."

"Good. And you'll be getting a call from Mrs. Boone's daughter and son-in-law. They just bought land out by Miller's Pond and want to build a house." She nudged him with her elbow. "See, I told you we could handle being partners."

He laughed. "Right. Partners who rarely work together." He built, she fixed up or tore down. And she was damned good at her job, too, thank God. She had restored his spontaneous nature and repaired his ability to forgive. Only Cassie would have chipped away at his defenses until he understood no one was put on this earth to be alone. Yes, life was uncertain, but to *not* get attached to anything or anyone wasn't really living.

"We're a team, a family, Tanner, and that's what counts. Besides, with this huge place, we'll always have projects to work on together at home."

"I'm sure the next project will be cleanup. It'll take days. You must have invited the whole town," he teased.

"Of course. But I know you're not complaining, because the alternative would be for everyone to come on their own, which would mean nonstop company—"

"The open house is a great idea." Still, he missed

having her to himself. The buzz of the crowd continued, but he ignored it. He nuzzled her neck and she leaned into him.

"I've got a surprise for you, Tanner. Mom is taking the baby home with her for a little while and Georgie offered to come tomorrow and help with cleanup, so...I was thinking, we never did finish carving our initials under the stairs."

"That's great, but who knows how long it'll take to clear this place out?"

"Who said we had to wait?"

He grinned and briefly wondered how many other wives would rendezvous with their husbands in the middle of their own party, then quickly decided he didn't care. He was one lucky man. "How soon?"

"I'll get the diaper bag, see them off, then meet you by the closet door."

He hugged the woman responsible for bringing love back into his life. For so many years, he'd never allowed himself to dream of a home or family. Now, he couldn't imagine living without either one. "I'm counting the minutes," he whispered, and silently vowed to spend the rest of his days trying to make her as happy as she had made him.

* * * * *

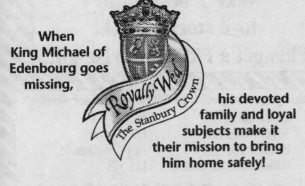

This Mother's Day
Give Your Mom
A Royal Treat

Win a fabulous one-week vacation in Puerto Rico for you and your mother at the luxurious Inter-Continental San Juan Resort & Casino. The prize includes round trip airfare for two, breakfast daily and a mother and daughter day of beauty at the beachfront hotel's spa.

INTER·CONTINENTAL
San Juan
RESORT & CASINO

Here's all you have to do:

Tell us in 100 words or less how your mother helped with the romance in your life. It may be a story about your engagement, wedding or those boyfriends when you were a teenager or any other romantic advice from your mother. The entry will be judged based on its originality, emotionally compelling nature and sincerity. See official rules on following page.

Send your entry to:
Mother's Day Contest

In Canada
P.O. Box 637
Fort Erie, Ontario
L2A 5X3

In U.S.A.
P.O. Box 9076
3010 Walden Ave.
Buffalo, NY
14269-9076

Or enter online at www.eHarlequin.com

All entries must be postmarked by April 1, 2002.
Winner will be announced May 1, 2002. Contest open to Canadian and U.S. residents who are 18 years of age and older. No purchase necessary to enter. Void where prohibited.

PRROY

Two ways to enter:

- **Via The Internet:** Log on to the Harlequin romance website (www.eHarlequin.com) anytime beginning 12:01 a.m. E.S.T., January 1, 2002 through 11:59 p.m. E.S.T., April 1, 2002 and follow the directions displayed on-line to enter your name, address (including zip code), e-mail address and in 100 words or fewer, describe how your mother helped with the romance in your life.

- **Via Mail:** Handprint (or type) on an 8 1/2" x 11" plain piece of paper, your name, address (including zip code) and e-mail address (if you have one), and in 100 words or fewer, describe how your mother helped with the romance in your life. Mail your entry via first-class mail to: Harlequin Mother's Day Contest 2216, (in the U.S.) P.O. Box 9076, Buffalo, NY 14269-9076; (in Canada) P.O. Box 637, Fort Erie, Ontario, Canada L2A 5X3.

For eligibility, entries must be submitted either through a completed Internet transmission or postmarked no later than 11:59 p.m. E.S.T., April 1, 2002 (mail-in entries must be received by April 9, 2002). Limit one entry per person, household address and e-mail address. On-line and/or mailed entries received from persons residing in geographic areas in which entry is not permissible will be disqualified.

Entries will be judged by a panel of judges, consisting of members of the Harlequin editorial, marketing and public relations staff using the following criteria:
- Originality - 50%
- Emotional Appeal - 25%
- Sincerity - 25%

In the event of a tie, duplicate prizes will be awarded. Decisions of the judges are final.

Prize: A 6-night/7-day stay for two at the Inter-Continental San Juan Resort & Casino, including round-trip coach air transportation from gateway airport nearest winner's home (approximate retail value: $4,000). Prize includes breakfast daily and a mother and daughter day of beauty at the beachfront hotel's spa. Prize consists of only those items listed as part of the prize. Prize is valued in U.S. currency.

All entries become the property of Torstar Corp. and will not be returned. No responsibility is assumed for lost, late, illegible, incomplete, inaccurate, non-delivered or misdirected mail or misdirected e-mail, for technical, hardware or software failures of any kind, lost or unavailable network connections, or failed, incomplete, garbled or delayed computer transmission or any human error which may occur in the receipt or processing of the entries in this Contest.

Contest open only to residents of the U.S. (except Colorado) and Canada, who are 18 years of age or older and is void wherever prohibited by law; all applicable laws and regulations apply. Any litigation within the Province of Quebec respecting the conduct or organization of a publicity contest may be submitted to the Régie des alcools, des courses et des jeux for a ruling. Any litigation respecting the awarding of a prize may be submitted to the Régie des alcools, des courses et des jeux only for the purpose of helping the parties reach a settlement. Employees and immediate family members of Torstar Corp. and D.L. Blair, Inc., their affiliates, subsidiaries and all other agencies, entities and persons connected with the use, marketing or conduct of this Contest are not eligible to enter. Taxes on prize are the sole responsibility of winner. Acceptance of any prize offered constitutes permission to use winner's name, photograph or other likeness for the purposes of advertising, trade and promotion on behalf of Torstar Corp., its affiliates and subsidiaries without further compensation to the winner, unless prohibited by law.

Winner will be determined no later than April 15, 2002 and will be notified by mail. Winner will be required to sign and return an Affidavit of Eligibility form within 15 days after winner notification. Non-compliance within that time period may result in disqualification and an alternate winner may be selected. Winner of trip must execute a Release of Liability prior to ticketing and must possess required travel documents (e.g. Passport, photo ID) where applicable. Travel must be completed within 12 months of selection and is subject to traveling companion completing and returning a Release of Liability prior to travel; and hotel and flight accommodations availability. Certain restrictions and blackout dates may apply. No substitution of prize permitted by winner. Torstar Corp. and D.L. Blair, Inc., their parents, affiliates, and subsidiaries are not responsible for errors in printing or electronic presentation of Contest, or entries. In the event of printing or other errors which may result in unintended prize values or duplication of prizes, all affected entries shall be null and void. If for any reason the Internet portion of the Contest is not capable of running as planned, including infection by computer virus, bugs, tampering, unauthorized intervention, fraud, technical failures, or any other causes beyond the control of Torstar Corp. which corrupt or affect the administration, secrecy, fairness, integrity or proper conduct of the Contest, Torstar Corp. reserves the right, at its sole discretion, to disqualify any individual who tampers with the entry process and to cancel, terminate, modify or suspend the Contest or the Internet portion thereof. In the event the Internet portion must be terminated a notice will be posted on the website and all entries received prior to termination will be judged in accordance with these rules. In the event of a dispute regarding an on-line entry, the entry will be deemed submitted by the authorized holder of the e-mail account submitted at the time of entry. Authorized account holder is defined as the natural person who is assigned to an e-mail address by an Internet access provider, on-line service provider or other organization that is responsible for arranging e-mail address for the domain associated with the submitted e-mail address. Torstar Corp. and/or D.L. Blair Inc. assumes no responsibility for any computer injury or damage related to or resulting from accessing and/or downloading any sweepstakes material. Rules are subject to any requirements/limitations imposed by the FCC. Purchase or acceptance of a product offer does not improve your chances of winning.

For winner's name (available after May 1, 2002), send a self-addressed, stamped envelope to: Harlequin Mother's Day Contest Winners 2216, P.O. Box 4200 Blair, NE 68009-4200 or you may access the www.eHarlequin.com Web site through June 3, 2002.

Contest sponsored by Torstar Corp., P.O. Box 9042, Buffalo, NY 14269-9042.